ALSO BY CHRISTINE CONRADT

Pregnant at 17

Murdered at 17

CHRISTINE CONRADT

An Imprint of HarperCollins*Publishers*

HarperTeen is an imprint of HarperCollins Publishers.

Missing at 17
Copyright © 2018 by Christine Conradt

Library of Congress Control Number: 2017959280
ISBN 978-0-06-265164-8

Typography by Jenna Stempel
18 19 20 21 22   PC/LSCH   10 9 8 7 6 5 4 3 2 1

First Edition

To Mom and Dad, for supporting my dreams
and for not putting me up for adoption during those
turbulent teenage years. And to my sister, Jenn,
for not ratting me out to Mom and Dad, even though
the peach-flavored gum wasn't fooling anyone.
You are all extraordinary, and so is your love.

missing at 17

ONE
SOUR CANDY

"You are *not* going to believe what I just heard." Avery, breathless with excitement, darted through the throng of teenagers drifting down the hall of the high school, on her way to Candace's locker. Avery Wilkes was petite and fragile with a shock of glossy black hair, and at this moment she was struggling to contain some important news.

"What?" Candace responded without taking her eyes off the mirror on her locker door. With a manicured nail she scraped the stray gloss from the corner of her full, pink lips. Candace White, nicknamed

"Candy" by her friends and family, was the type of girl who could look beautiful without trying. Her long blond hair cascaded down her back in languid waves and her eyelashes held a perfect, permanent curl that framed her big brown eyes like those of an innocent, newly born fawn.

But beneath the sun-splashed cheeks and ever so slightly turned-up nose, Candace was a brewing storm. There was this ever-present feeling that she simply didn't quite fit; a pervading sense that she was missing something much better out there and that while she lived her day-to-day life, her real life—the one she was meant to live—was passing her by someplace else.

Avery slapped her hand over the mirror, eager to get Candace's attention. "I'm serious, Candy. You're going to want to hear this."

Candace turned squarely to her best friend, feigning an interested look. Avery loved to be the bearer of news, any kind of news, and she had a habit of hyping mundane events into something seemingly interesting just for a few moments in the spotlight. Being a drama queen was one of Avery's few quirks, but Candace, having known Avery since junior high, didn't mind. In the grand scheme of their lives, Avery had never been anything but a great friend. She was loyal, sweet, and genuinely caring, but the glue that really held them together was Avery's ability to put up with Candace's moods without getting offended. Candace was well aware that she could blow at any second. When she did, it was like a dam breaking. Venom-laced words would come gushing out until she ran dry.

Candace always felt guilty afterward. Each time it happened, she'd loathe herself for days until she could accept her own promise that it wouldn't happen again. But it always happened again. This flaw made it difficult for people to really get close to Candace and she knew this, but it never seemed to matter with Avery. Avery knew below-the-surface Candace was a good person.

"I'm listening! I can do two things at once. I'm smart like that." Candace plucked Avery's hand from the mirror, giving her room to check her mascara.

Avery lowered her voice and glanced from side to side, letting the suspense build. "Let's just say . . . Ian doesn't waste much time." *Now* she had Candy's attention. For real. "He's seeing Jenny Martin," Avery continued. "The sophomore."

Candace's big brown eyes grew even bigger.

"That volleyball chick?"

"Yup. I guess they hooked up at Dane's party the other night."

Candace slammed her locker door shut with more force than necessary. She'd never been sucker-punched but she thought this is what it must feel like. For a few seconds she actually forgot to breathe as images of her ex-boyfriend walking hand in hand with the lanky Jenny Martin flashed through her mind in rapid succession. Candace was at a loss for words. All she could come up with was "That was quick."

How could he want to be with someone so soon? she wondered, a hot, uncomfortable feeling rising from the pit of her stomach. They'd just broken up. Literally. Last week. And in that span of time, she'd had a helluva time getting Ian out of her head. No matter what she did, her thoughts drifted back to time they'd spent together, events they'd attended as a couple, moments that at one point, meant something. Even mundane things she'd thought she'd forgotten—a good-luck kiss before one of Ian's basketball games or the sneaking of midnight phone calls on school nights—popped up in her mind at the oddest times, interrupting her concentration on anything else. *Apparently Ian doesn't have that problem,* she thought. She was trying hard to ignore the stinging in her eyes that comes in those seconds just before you start to cry.

"It makes sense he'd go out with someone two years younger. Considering how immature he is," Avery muttered, folding her arms and shaking her head. "You'd think he could at least wait a week, though."

"I don't care what he does," Candace said under her breath. Her tone was convincing but Avery knew better; Candace cared more than she was letting on.

Two hours later, as Candace was making her way from European History where their teacher, Mr. Rafael, surprised them with a pop quiz she was sure she failed, Candace saw something she wished she hadn't. Ian's tall and gangly six-one frame was standing at the top of the stairs. His oversize hands, which made him a formidable forward guard on the varsity basketball team, were cupped on each side of Jenny Martin's freckled face, their mouths inches apart. Candace couldn't help but stare at Ian's mess of thick, curly hair with streaky blond highlights tilted to the right as he leaned in to plant a soft, slow kiss on Jenny's lips.

A wave of emotion came over Candace as she watched Jenny, the youngest player on the girls' volleyball team, awkwardly rest her hands on Ian's waist as they shared an inappropriately intimate public kiss. Then, somehow, an inner strength kicked in and Candace felt detached, as if she were observing two total strangers desperately trying to connect. It was almost disgusting how he unnaturally kept that kiss going, twisting his head back and forth long after it should have ended. Then it dawned on Candace that Ian used to kiss her like that, when they first started dating. It was obnoxious how he couldn't just give a simple kiss and then pull away like normal people do. His kisses always went on longer than they needed to and his timing was god-awful. As his tongue would dart in and out of her mouth, sweeping from side to side, she sometimes pictured him as a doctor swabbing her mouth like the time she'd had strep throat.

After four months of dating seriously, Candace had felt much more comfortable with Ian. There was a level of openness—and freedom to say whatever was on her mind. It was liberating. But like most things, Candace didn't know when to quit. She hadn't learned yet to temper the privilege of raw honesty with sensitivity to other people's feelings. Never in a million years had she intended to hurt him, but when Ian playfully pulled her behind the Monster Monsoon waterslide at Ocean World Park on a particularly hot summer day, buried his fingers into her wet hair and began to twist his tongue around in her mouth, Candace had decided it was finally time to be honest. *Holy crap*, she thought as his tongue flipped from side to side like a minnow on a fishing line. *Is he trying to spell the entire alphabet?*

"Ian," she said as she pulled away.

"What's wrong?" he asked, his eyes showing concern.

"I'm not trying to be mean or anything, but . . . how about if I kiss you this time?"

Ian looked confused. "Isn't that what we were just doing?"

"No, I mean more like this. . . ." She slid her hands over his bare chest, stood on her tiptoes, and gave him a short but passionate kiss, keeping her tongue in her own mouth. He didn't respond and when they parted, she smiled. "See? Wasn't that better than a tongue war?"

Ian deflated a little. "Oh."

She could see that he was truly wounded by her suggestion, and immediately felt guilty for saying anything at all. She certainly didn't want Ian to be self-conscious about the way he kissed, or worse yet, avoid kissing her altogether. She liked that he was so affectionate, especially in public, and now what had she done? As usual, her mouth had gotten her into trouble and maybe screwed up their relationship for good.

"Ian, if I hurt your feelings I'm sorry. I didn't mean to. I just . . . I think you and I have different ways of kissing."

"We can kiss any way you want," he said flatly, making her feel even worse. As he started to walk back toward the wave pool, she grabbed his hand. A shiver came over her and she could feel goose bumps forming on her arms and legs as she pulled him back into the shade of the waterslide's massive overhead tube.

"Don't be mad." She tugged on his arm playfully, hoping to lighten the mood. Ian sighed and pulled her into an embrace. She clung to his warm skin as his arms wrapped around her back.

"Some things are just harder than they should be," he said.

"No they're not," she assured him, unsure if he meant their kissing, the relationship, or both. Deep down, she suspected he meant both but she'd waited so long to have a boyfriend, especially one as cute as Ian, she didn't even want to let her mind explore the idea that there might be too many things between them that didn't line up. Every time she felt the same way, she pushed the thought aside and reminded herself how great it felt when he draped his arm around her shoulders. "Things are great." Her tone wasn't as convincing as she'd hoped it would be. Ian nodded, still feeling cut down as Candace silently berated herself for bringing up the kissing problem at all. For the sake of salvaging the date and the money they'd spent on full-day admission to the water park, Ian got over it and after kissing the top of her head, suggested they snag a two-person raft for the Tsunami Twist. Upon splashing into the overly chlorinated catch pool at the bottom of the Tsunami's eight-foot final drop, they were laughing and joking and trying to dunk each other just like they had earlier in the day. In that moment, things seemed the same to Candace, but it wasn't lost on her that Ian never kissed her quite as passionately after that day.

As she turned away from Ian and Jenny, who were now gazing lovingly into each other's eyes as if they were two lovers who'd finally reunited after walking the earth for centuries trying to find each other, Candace exhaled a loud sigh. She'd screwed up that relationship beyond repair, and she had to take some of the blame for making Ian want to spend time with someone else—someone who appreciated his epic-length, Oliver-Stone-director's-cut-style French kiss.

Candace stalked off to her next class in a fog of resentment, sure that Ian had started seeing Jenny before he broke up with her over the weekend. In a text, no less. *What kind of a guy breaks up with someone in a text?* she thought. A spineless tool who spends his time running basketball drills and bragging about how he could hold his own in the NBA. Screw him, screw his sloppy kisses, and screw the undefeated-yet-overrated girls' volleyball team.

In Biology, Candace dropped her books onto her desk and plopped into her seat, the thought of Ian and Jenny lip-locked in the middle of the hallway stuck in her mind. Every bone in her body wanted to leap from her chair, march right into the boys' locker room, and punch Ian in the face. When she noticed her hands were clenched into fists, she forced herself to flatten them on her desk. *Stop being so angry*, she silently ordered. *Focus on whatever stupid crap we're doing in this class today. Thoughts of beating Ian to a pulp will only distract you.*

Realizing it wasn't much of a pep talk, she decided to

try something different. Sitting up straight, she closed her eyes, inhaled, and touched the tips of her forefingers to the tips of her thumbs on each hand. This was called the *Om mudra* and she'd learned it from a yoga class that her mother had dragged her to a few times hoping it would help her mellow out. The idea behind the *Om mudra* was to create a circle for the energy to flow back into the brain and somehow relax you. Realizing she might look like a freak, Candace tucked her *Om* hands below her desk and exhaled.

Thoughts immediately went to a happy time . . . with Ian. *Dammit.*

Last Wednesday night, they'd been sitting on the beach in Santa Monica, staring out at the flocks of tourists crowding the pier. It was perfect. The faint strains of carnival music, the salty smell of the cool ocean breeze, the reflection of the Ferris wheel's colorful lights glistening in the surf. Sitting on the sand, their shoes lined up next to each other, Candace took a deep breath and looked out at the inky darkness. She cradled the little stuffed puppy in her arms that Ian had won for her at the basketball toss booth. As she delicately fingered its felt collar and the button eye that was already loose, it felt good to just sit with Ian and not say a word. Candace felt her thoughts slow down, the emotions that constantly swirled inside her settle. She didn't have to think about her grades—which weren't particularly good. Or the fact that her mother kept harping on how she'd never get into college if she didn't bring up her GPA. She didn't have to miss her father, who moved out of the house two years ago after her parents got divorced. She didn't think about her younger brother, Andrew. She loved him, but thirteen-year-old boys can be a handful and Andrew certainly was. A few weeks ago, she'd spent ten minutes on the phone with Avery before she discovered him hiding in her closet eavesdropping. But that was someplace else now, far away. In this moment, there was no annoying mother, no absent father, no snooper-trooper little brother. There was just her and Ian and an ocean that stretched on forever into the black calm.

"What are you thinking about?" Ian asked as he let a handful of cool sand slip through his fingers and cover her feet. She smiled.

"Nothing important," she said, and took his hand. Ian lay down in the sand beside her and pressed his body against hers. As he wrapped his arms around her, she interlocked their fingers and gazed up at the moon.

Soft, she thought. Everything felt soft: the sand laced with tiny smooth pebbles, the cotton of Ian's worn-out T-shirt, the subtle breeze that caught a few strands of her hair and sent them dancing over her face. She even felt soft on the inside, as if there was no skin separating her from the outside world. Everything just flowed through her. She wished she could keep that feeling inside her forever, carry it with her, retreat to it when someone pissed her off or when she felt like the lone puzzle piece tucked in the far corner of the closet long after the puzzle had been finished and discarded. *Yes, this is what harmony feels like*, she thought. *This is happiness.*

But not today.

Today, plain-faced, boring, ponytailed Jenny Martin was happy. Candace was not. *I'm not what Ian wants.* Her fingers released the stupid *Om mudra* position that never worked anyway. *I will never have that tranquility and sense of belonging again.*

"Don't forget that the first allele is dominant and the second is recessive. . . ." Ms. West's voice pulled Candace out of her daydream. Candace looked up to see Ms. West pointing at a genetics chart with her left hand, holding the point a little too long. Avery was sure that this behavior only started after Ms. West, on the downhill side of her thirties, showed up to school after summer vacation this year wearing a very large rock on her ring finger. It was obnoxiously large. And it occasionally sparkled in a way that Candace wondered if anyone had ever gone blind from. After a long discussion, both Candace and Avery agreed that (1) Ms. West must've landed herself someone with some serious cash, (2) it was probably a blood diamond that had been dragged out of a diamond mine somewhere in Africa on the chest of a dead miner who had lost his life searching for a diamond of that caliber, and (3) Ms. West suddenly felt the need to point at everything she could with her left hand even though she was right-handed.

Alleles . . . dominant alleles . . . Candace scrawled the words into her notebook to appear as if she were listening. She outlined the word "dominant." Maybe Ian wanted someone less dominant, she thought. Someone who goes with the flow . . . is less argumentative . . . or maybe he just wants someone more sporty and athletic. His text was pretty vague.

Candy, I care a lot about you but this relationship isn't working for me. Even if we're not a couple, I'll always be here if you need me. Sorry to do this in a text btw.

"What the hell?" Candace had immediately punched out his number on her phone even though she had it saved in speed dial. It rang only once before she heard his lame voice mail message come on, proof that he was sitting right there, staring at her name that popped up, and instead of answering, pressed ignore.

The only thing that hurt more than being broken up with by a text is being ignored. How could he ignore her? After all the times he'd said he loved her? After she loaned him a hundred dollars—her birthday money from her grandparents that she'd planned to use on a new purse she'd been saving for, so he could avoid telling his dad he'd lost the money his father'd given him for school supplies? After she'd made him an entire pot of chicken noodle soup—well, chicken spaghetti soup, when he caught a cold last March? What an ungrateful jerk.

Stop! Stop thinking about him! Candace dug her fingernails into her scalp trying to bleed the thoughts of Ian from her mind. Alleles . . . dominant alleles . . .

"So you see . . . it's impossible for two people with blue eyes to have a child with brown eyes because brown is dominant and blue is recessive," Ms. West pointed out on the chart, her ring finger slightly elevated above the rest.

Wait. What? Candace thought. She must've missed something there. Two blue-eyed people can't have a brown-eyed kid? That's not true. Both of her parents had blue eyes and she had brown. Had she found a flaw in the curriculum? Was Ms. West so busy planning her wedding that she hadn't done her research?

Candace raised her hand with confidence.

"Yes, Candace?"

"That's not true. Both my parents have blue eyes and I have brown." When Ms. West paused, Candace initially thought she had her.

"Are you sure about their eye color? Because bio-logically speaking, that's not possible."

From the back of the room, career goof-off and chronic attention-seeker Joey Jones blurted out, "Maybe you're adopted!" Laughter erupted from half of the students. The other half rolled their eyes, determined not to encourage Joey. Candace, hiding embarrassment with attitude, shot Joey a poisonous look. So did Avery.

Candace realized she hadn't seen her father in almost a month but she was one hundred percent sure he had blue eyes. So did her mother. The book, or Ms. West, or the state of California's Department of Education was wrong. But now that everyone was staring at her, and Ms. West was challenging her claim, Candace knew she had to substantiate it.

"Just like sometimes babies are born with blue eyes and then they turn a different color later on. Right?" Candace said with a little attitude, refusing to abandon her position and give Joey the last word. Her neighbors Colin and Sadie had four kids, and when they brought the last one home around Christmastime, Candace, Andrew, and their mother had gone over to see the baby and bring the family a lasagna. Candace had been sitting right there, holding the tiny-headed infant in her lap, when her mom and Sadie had discussed how the baby's eye color would change. *Boo-yah, Ms. West. Take that.*

"That can happen," Ms. West responded carefully. "But it has nothing to do with recessive genes. Caucasian babies are often born with blue eyes but that's just because their irises may gain more pigment as they develop."

Before Candace could respond, Joey blurted out, "You're totally adopted, Candy!" The students that had laughed before, laughed even harder. Candace felt her face turn crimson.

"That's enough," Ms. West warned. "Let's get back to the lesson."

Candace could sense the lingering stares as the fiery red humiliation tried to push through her skin and escape through her pores. Why in the world did she say that? Rule number one: Never reveal any personal information in a classroom setting. Rule number two: She couldn't remember the second rule, but it wasn't important now anyway. She'd have to spend the next several months quelling rumors she'd been adopted. Between Ian and this, it was too much. Too much for one day. Candace slammed her book shut and jumped to her feet.

"What you're teaching is a lie!" Candace yelled out, scooping up her papers and book. "I'm not gonna sit here and listen to someone who doesn't know what the hell she's talking about!" By the time the last word was out, Candace was halfway to the door. She didn't even notice the stunned silence that fell over the room or the shocked look on Ms. West's face. She didn't notice Avery, who started to stand up and follow her until Ms. West put up a hand signaling to let her go. All Candace cared about was getting the hell out of there. She yanked open the door, stalked out of the room, and left the entire ordeal behind her.

Her hands were shaking so badly by the time she

made it to her locker, it took two tries at the combination before Candace could open it and shove her books inside. Tears began to well in her eyes as the anger flooded through her: anger at herself for having another outburst in class, anger at Joey Jones for being a class-A jerk, and anger at Ian for choosing a five-ten sophomore over her. All she wanted was to be far away from all of it. If only she could walk out of the school and never, ever come back.

Tugging hard at the paisley print straps of her backpack, Candace crossed the campus to the student lot where her red Honda was parked, without taking her eyes off the ground. She didn't want to see or talk to anyone. All she wanted to do was drive as far away as her two-door Accord would take her. But when she stuffed her key in the ignition and turned it hard, she could hear the engine sputter without turning over.

"Damn it to hell!" she screamed, as she smacked her palms repeatedly on the steering wheel. "I hate my life!"

She pulled the key out and tried again. This time the engine coughed briefly before firing up. Throwing the transmission into reverse, Candace stepped on the gas, causing her Honda to lurch backward, barely missing the bumper of the car parked behind her. With a squeal of her tires, Candace was out of the lot and on her way home to confront the one woman who knew the truth—her mother.

TWO
AN UNTIMELY TRUTH

Candace threw open the door and marched past the stairs, through the spotless living room, and like a whirlwind, entered the kitchen where Andrew was placing frozen chicken nuggets onto a baking sheet. He looked up, almost frightened.

"Where's Mom?!"

"I'm right here, honey." Candace's mother, Shannon, hurried into the room from the hallway, concerned by her daughter's tone. "What's wrong?" Shannon was still wiping her petite hands on the plush gray towel that hung in the powder room.

"I hate school! I'm dropping out!" Candace said as she heaved her backpack onto the counter.

"Can anyone say *PMS*?" Andrew muttered, taking advantage of any opportunity to tease his sister. Candace ignored him. His quips were the least of her problems.

"What happened, sweetie?" Her mother set the towel aside, her angular chin tilting slightly to the left the way it always did when she was worried.

"I got into an argument with stupid Ms. West! But it wasn't just her. It was the whole class!" Candace could tell from her mother's reaction that she was secretly hoping her daughter didn't get expelled. They both knew it wasn't beyond the realm of possibility.

"None of the stuff she was teaching was true! It got out of control and I called her a liar and walked out."

Andrew let his jaw drop, intentionally being dramatic. "You called your teacher a liar in front of the class?!"

Candace pretended not to hear him. She was genuinely upset, and Andrew had a hard time taking anything seriously. "It was terrible."

"Slow down," her mother said, stepping closer. "Tell me what happened."

Candace relayed the story about how Ms. West kept saying it was impossible for two blue-eyed parents to have a brown-eyed daughter and how Joey made some wisecrack about how she was adopted.

"So I said that a lot of babies are born with blue eyes and then they turn brown and she said that has to do with their eyeballs developing and not genetics and she's wrong! Right?!"

As she spoke, Candace saw her mother pick up the towel she'd just put down and nervously dry her hands. When she finished asking the question, her mom was silent. "What I said is true, isn't it?" Candace asked with increasing concern.

Her mom finally nodded. "I suppose it is."

"Well that has to be it, because I'm *not* adopted!" Candace announced it as if the mere declaration could make it true. But deep down, the question had blazed inside her brain the entire drive home. What if that idiot Joey was right and she really was adopted? What if she'd lived her whole life believing that Shannon and Kurt were her biological parents and it turned out they'd been stringing her along with seventeen years of lies?

Candace could see the pain in her mother's eyes,

and when her mother finally looked down at the countertop and bit her bottom lip, Candace involuntarily stepped back, putting distance between them.

"Oh my god. I'm not, am I?"

As Candace uttered the question, she already knew from her mother's reaction that her fears were about to come true. Still, she needed to hear it for herself.

Candace gasped as her mom abruptly walked out of the room. She turned to Andrew, who just stared back at her in confused silence. This was unusual behavior for her mother and both of them knew it. Shannon's worst fault was how she dealt with difficult situations; she became irrationally defensive. And that was when she was right! When she was wrong, she could rarely admit it. Her temper would flare and she'd say things she didn't mean and later regretted. Her mother exercised self-control with her children, but they were the only two immune.

Shannon's temper had been a point of contention with their father. He'd been the target of their mom's frequent outbursts and, Candace observed that over time, that caused their dad to work more and more. He took on more transatlantic flights, which kept him out of the house for longer periods. It may have given both her parents a reprieve from each other, but it fed their mom's complaints about their father's waning involvement with his family. Those late-night arguments in angry whispers that Candace would catch snippets of on her way to the bathroom did little to entice their dad to spend more time at home. Candace quickly flashed back to when she found out her parents were getting a divorce.

In October of the previous year, Candace's father came home from a long flight from Hong Kong and went to bed. The next day, as he was driving Candace to school, he was completely silent. Normally he listened to talk radio in the morning, chuckling to himself and throwing a grin to Candace each time the show's hosts made some witty little quip. But on that particular day, he hadn't even turned it on. Instead, he'd stared through the windshield preoccupied, his square jaw taut. Candace knew something wasn't right. As he pulled up to the curb to let her out, she hesitated.

"Everything okay, Dad?" she asked.

"Have you ever heard that saying 'The darkest time of night is right before the dawn'?" he responded, looking her straight in the eye. Candace had never heard that saying before and wasn't absolutely sure what it meant. She nodded anyway, hoping he'd just tell her what was wrong.

"Even when things seem bad in the moment, or . . . things change and it feels like they're changing for the worst, that's when new and better things usually happen. Does that make sense?"

"Not really. That's kinda vague," Candace said honestly.

"Do you remember when you were nine and you really wanted to go to summer camp but then you fell off your bike and sprained your wrist and couldn't go?" he asked, and she nodded. "You were so upset about missing camp and having to stay home but . . . because you were home, we ended up taking you to the concert in the park and that's where you found that man's wallet and turned it in and he gave you a hundred dollars as a reward. Remember?"

"What does any of this have to do with right now?" Candace's heart was still in her throat, waiting for her father to tell her what was really on his mind.

"I'm just saying that sometimes things don't turn out the way we think they will, but it's still okay. That's all I'm saying. It's just something to keep in mind as you go through your day and through your life. I'm going to try to keep it in mind too." He looked down after he said it.

Candace had always felt a special connection to her father. She could tell in this moment that whatever was weighing on his mind was very, very heavy.

"Is there something you want to tell me?" It was the same thing he always said to her when she seemed stressed.

Her father's tense features relaxed a little, and he squeezed her arm lovingly. "No, honey. I just want you to always keep an open mind."

She decided not to press. That tactic never worked on her father. Candace had seen his reaction when her mother kept digging at him to talk when he didn't want to. One of the reasons her father shared important things with her was because she was able to do what her mom couldn't seem to do—just listen. As Candace got out of the car, that familiar feeling of not belonging was stronger than ever. She wasn't sure what her dad was talking about or what unexpected, seemingly bad but potentially good thing was about to happen, but whatever it was, she was convinced that being at school was a waste of time.

Later that night, when they all sat down at the

dinner table over Chinese takeout, Candace found out what the ambiguous discussion with her father was all about.

"So, your mother and I have something to tell you," her dad uttered. Andrew, totally oblivious to their father's rigid tone, looked up from his kung pao chicken with happy anticipation.

"You're getting a divorce, aren't you?" Candace asked flatly. The moment of silence afterward seemed to hover over the table like a thunderhead. Andrew's expression was the only one that changed.

"Wait, what?" he asked. "Candy's not right, is she?"

Their mother, unable to keep her emotions in check, looked to the ceiling and dabbed her eye with the corner of her napkin.

"We are," their dad said softly. "We've discussed it and we're both certain that it's the best thing for everyone."

An unexpected wave of relief washed over Candace as tears formed in Andrew's eyes.

"Please don't," Andrew begged, fighting back the desperation as he tried to reason with his parents. "I want you to stay together." Andrew's words hung in the air. Her mother and father just looked down, neither willing to answer.

Candace wasn't particularly stunned by the news. She was quite aware of the fact that her parents' relationship had been strained for a long time. Neither one of them was happy. The moment her dad would walk in the door, her mom would start bitching. Now it had finally happened. Her mother had driven her father to leave. That's what her father had been trying to tell her to keep an open mind about earlier. She felt completely detached from the situation as she observed her little brother pleading his case. She sort of tuned the whole thing out, lost in her own thoughts about the logistics of having parents that didn't reside under the same roof.

As Andrew abruptly got up and marched to his room, their mother followed him. Candace, now alone with her dad, looked over at him. She could tell by the way he was running his hands through his thick hair that he felt conflicted. He didn't speak.

"Can I live with you?" Candace asked. Kurt turned to her, surprised.

"You mean, instead of with your mom?"

Candace nodded, assuming he'd agree without hesitating. Instead, he paused.

"Your mother and I will need to work out the details, but we're both going to be just as much a part of your lives as we've always been."

"She said I have to stay here, didn't she?" Candace pressed, sure that her mother was using her as a pawn to punish her father.

"No, but it does make sense, Candy. Your school's here. And I'm gone all the time for work."

"But Mom and I fight all the time," Candace said, surprising herself at how steady her voice was. The truth was, she felt no emotion at all. It was as if all of this was happening to someone else.

"I think . . ." her father said, and ran his forefinger and thumb around his mouth slowly. "I think things will get better between you two without me here. Our relationship has created a lot of stress that I'm sure has spilled over onto you and Andrew."

"What does that even mean? Are you saying you don't want me?"

"Not at all," he said sternly. "But your mother feels that this is the best environment for you, and I agree with her." Of course she did, Candace thought. How could her mother keep control of Candace's life if Candace was living with her dad?

Candace looked down at the greasy egg roll and bits of chicken that sat, untouched, on her plate. They'd ordered the same Chinese takeout a million times from the little Mandarin restaurant that sat dead center in the middle of a cheesy strip mall at the edge of their neighborhood. They'd sat at their table a million times as a family, talking about Andrew's latest achievement or the movie set her mother was working on or some crazy first-class passenger on her dad's most recent flight. A million mundane conversations over barely above-average egg foo yong and broccoli beef. And now, here that food was, the backdrop to one of the most life-altering conversations her family had ever had. Didn't an announcement this monumental deserve something a little more special? Maybe not. Maybe this is how life is, Candace thought. Major life changes happening over boring, sticky white rice. She pictured Mr. Lee, who owned the Chinese restaurant. Did he ever suspect as he was standing in his cramped little kitchen, sweating under a white paper hat as he stir-fried their vegetables in his oversize wok, that the meal he was making might be the last one her family ever had together at the same table? Would he be flattered that they chose his food to be the food that sat on their plates as they made such an important announcement?

These are not the things I should be thinking about right now, Candace thought. *My parents have decided to dismantle our entire lives and I'm thinking about Mr. Lee and his Chinese food. There is clearly something wrong with me.*

That detached feeling Candace had the night her parents announced their divorce was one hundred percent different than what she was feeling right now. To see her mother silently exit the room struck fear in Candace's heart. Fear like she'd never felt before. Fear like the bottom was dropping out underneath her very feet and she had no idea how far she'd fall or if she'd survive the landing.

Candace had expected her mother to assure her that Ms. West was nothing more than a subpar teacher who couldn't keep her facts straight, that Candace was right for standing up to her, and that under no circumstances was she adopted. But her mother's reaction was different from anything she'd ever seen before.

When Candace and Andrew entered the living room, their mother was seated on the sofa, staring down at the coffee table. "Mom, what's going on?" Candace demanded.

"Honey, I don't know how to answer your question," her mom said, wiping away a tear before it could escape.

"What do you mean you don't know how? It's a

simple freaking question. Answer it! Just tell me I'm not adopted!"

"This isn't . . ." Her mother paused, searching for the words. "This isn't how I wanted any of this to come out. . . ."

Candace swallowed, horrified. "What?"

As her mother reached for her arm, Candace pulled away. She didn't even realize she'd done it. "Candace, sweetie . . . you know how much your dad and I love you. . . ."

"I'm adopted?" Candace looked straight into her mother's eyes, hoping for a different answer this time. Her voice was weaker than it had been before. Her mom hesitated a moment, then simply nodded. Candace felt as if her breath had been sucked out of her. She glanced over at Andrew, who looked like he could barely believe what he was hearing either.

"I wanted to tell you earlier, but—"

"You *wanted* to tell me?!" Candace blurted out. "Then why didn't you? How could you lie to me all this time?" In the moment, that was the biggest blow: the fact her parents had lied to her for so many years. Were they going to keep something this big a secret from her forever?

"We didn't see it as lying to you, honey! We just

wanted to find the right way to say it," her mother uttered, her voice laced with regret as she nervously tucked her blond hair behind her ear.

Candace wasn't having it. "You *lied* to me! You made me look like an idiot in front of my entire class! They all figured out that I'm adopted before I did!" Tears began to stream down Candace's cheeks. She just stood there, hoping her mother would suddenly leap up and laugh and say it was all a terrible joke, but that didn't happen.

"Am I adopted too?" Andrew asked, scared to hear the truth. The thought hadn't occurred to Candace. Maybe they had that in common. Deep inside her, there was a tiny flame of hope that both she and Andrew were in the same awful, uncomfortable situation. If they were, at least they were in it together.

Candace and Andrew both stared at their mother, waiting for an answer. After a moment, Shannon shook her head. "No."

No? So Andrew was their biological child and she wasn't?

"So it's just me? I'm the only one who doesn't belong in this family?" Candace shouted.

"You're a part of this family as much as your brother," her mom said, her voice level and heartfelt.

"But he's yours and I'm not! You should've told me the truth!"

Looking like she was consumed with guilt, her mother nodded. "I know. I'm sorry." Her mom tried to give Candace a hug, but Candace pushed her away.

"Don't touch me! I hate you! Can't you see that? I hate you and I hate everyone at that school! I'm never going back there!" Candace took a breath, trying to calm down as her mother looked on. And then it dawned on Candace that if she didn't belong here, she must belong somewhere else. "Who is my mom? My *real* mom?"

It took a few moments for her mother to answer. She seemed taken aback by the question.

"I never met her. I don't know who she is. . . ."

Upon hearing this, Candace abruptly rushed back into the kitchen where she grabbed her backpack and keys. She had no idea where she was going, but she couldn't stay there. Not one minute longer. She needed to be alone, to process, to think about what it all meant.

Andrew and their mother followed, looking worried.

"You don't hate *me*, though, right?" Andrew asked.

"I hate *everyone*!" There was venom in Candace's voice as she spun toward him, her eyes narrowing. The self-control she could usually muster to protect

Andrew's feelings was gone. She *was* angry at everyone and yes, she hated them all: her parents for lying to her every single day that they had pretended to be her real parents. Andrew for having what she'd always thought she had. And Ms. West for teaching everyone about alleles and recessive genes. She hated Joey for being the first person to speak the truth about her adoptive status. Her father for not being there to accuse. And most of all, she hated herself. She hated who she was, but who was that, really?

For years, Candace had observed her parents, subtly spotting characteristics in each of them that she also found in herself. Some were good, some weren't, but at least she had some idea where they came from. Now, what did she have? Absolutely nothing.

Candace was so busy grabbing her backpack, she didn't notice the rejection in her brother's eyes. "Candy, calm down!" Her mother tried to take control. "Don't say things you don't mean. . . ."

"I do mean it! I'm never coming back here again!" Candace yelled back as she raced out of the room, into the entryway, and threw open the front door. Her mother, without missing a beat, went after her, pursuing her all the way to Candace's car.

"Sweetie! Don't run off like this! We need to talk!"

"Don't you get it? I don't want to talk to you. Leave me alone!" As Candace opened the car door, her mom tried to grab the handle to keep her from pulling it shut. Candace managed to get it closed despite her mother's efforts, and pressed the lock. Shannon banged on the window with the palm of her hand for emphasis.

"Candace! I mean it! Get back in the house right now!"

"Don't tell me what to do. You're not my mother!" Candace spewed, trying hard to be as nasty and hurtful as she could.

From the look on her mom's face, her words hit the mark. Praying her car would start, Candace twisted the key and . . . yes! The engine roared to life! Relieved, Candace threw the car into reverse and peeled out of the driveway. As she slammed on the brake and shoved the transmission into drive, she saw her mother running down to the curb, waving her arms, hoping to convince Candace to stop. Candace didn't stop. She pressed hard on the gas and with a squeal of her tires, blasted off down the street. Before she turned the corner, she took one last look in her rearview and saw her mom standing in the middle of the street, holding her head, watching helplessly.

Alone in the car, Candace couldn't get her mind to stop racing. When the light turned green and the car in front didn't move as quickly as she wanted, she smashed her fist down on the horn, letting it blare at the car.

"Move it!"

The car rolled forward and changed lanes, allowing her to stomp down on the gas and speed past. She had no real destination in mind, but moving down the road felt better than sitting still. Maneuvering in and out of lanes, taking her anger out on drivers she passed, she grabbed her cell phone and recklessly dialed Avery's number. After a few rings, Avery's voice mail came on.

"I need to talk to you" was all Candace could manage to record. There was too much to launch into on a sixty-second voice mail. She needed to vent to her best friend in person. As soon as she hung up, her phone began to ring. Hoping it was Avery, she looked down at the display. Mom. Frustrated, Candace quickly pressed the ignore button and tossed the phone onto the passenger seat.

THREE
PRINCE CHARMING
WITH A FEW TATTOOS

Candace fished seven dollars and thirty-two cents from the bottom of her purse as she headed toward the entrance of the gas station. She was almost out of fuel, and though it wasn't a lot of money, at least it would get her a candy bar and another twenty or thirty miles. That's all she wanted right now: to be far, far away.

As she passed the row of pumps, she spotted a guy packing a box of cigarettes against the heel of his hand. Her mother hated smoking. She stepped into his path.

"Excuse me, could I bum one of those?"

The guy, apparently in a rush, let out a sigh and handed her a cigarette.

"Thanks," she said. The man hurried off toward his car and Candace stood there with an unlit cigarette in her hand, feeling awkward.

That's when she spotted him. A guy she'd never seen before. He'd just come around the corner of the building and was headed straight for her.

"'Scuse me, do you have a light?" she asked. The guy stopped and rubbed his chiseled jaw as he sized her up. At first he didn't say anything, which made her feel self-conscious, but she also had trouble looking away from his aqua-blue eyes. They seemed to draw her in.

He finally grinned and ran his fingers through his dirty-blond hair. "Rough day?" he asked with a smirk.

"Worst day ever," she replied, realizing her mascara had streaked down her face. Nervous, she twirled the cigarette between her fingers.

"Oh yeah? Why's that?" he asked, and crossed his muscular arms in front of his chest. As stunning as this guy was and as much as she had trouble looking away from his near-perfect white teeth and the hint of stubble that covered his chin, Candace didn't feel like getting into her life story.

"You don't have one of those pop-up lighter things in your car? I lost mine. . . ." she said as she nodded toward her Honda. He glanced in the direction of her nod, then pulled a Zippo lighter from the inside pocket of his leather jacket. He flipped it open and lit her cigarette with the dancing flame.

"Thanks," she said, and taking a long drag, started to walk away.

"Hey," the guy called after her. She turned back. "You didn't tell me why today's the worst day of your life."

"Can't smoke by the door," she said coyly, and continued to walk farther from the entrance, where she leaned back against the bricks under a fading lottery decal. She was surprised when he followed.

"Okay. *Now* tell me why you're having a bad day."

Candace was stuck. She'd run out of excuses. And there were worse things than this extremely hot guy standing in front of her, genuinely interested in why her life sucked.

"Well . . . it all started with my boyfriend, who dumped me last week, hanging all over some sophomore skank in the middle of the hall. Then, me getting into a fight with a teacher at school—which happens a lot—but this argument made me look like a complete idiot. I didn't know I was going to look like an idiot until I got home and my mom tells me she's not really my mom." As Candace finished, the guy covered his grin with his hand.

"So *that's* your *worst* day?" he asked. "An ex making out with some girl, a fight at school, and you're . . . *adopted*?"

"Go to hell," she said defensively, and took a drag off her cigarette. Hot Guy was making fun of her now. Of course he was, she thought. Par for the course.

"Whoa, easy there. I'm not making light of it." His voice dropped a note.

"Yes you were," she retorted. Who did this jerk think he was, anyway? She'd only known him for one minute and he was already poking fun at her? Screw him.

"All right. A little," he replied slowly. "But only because I'm adopted too." He shrugged.

Shocked, Candace snapped her head around to look up at him.

"You're adopted?" she said, her eyes narrowing with skepticism.

"Yeah," he assured her. "And it's not that big of a deal."

"It's a big deal for *me*," she said, and looked off across

the street, eager for the conversation to end. Candace just wanted to be alone to wallow in her sorrow and enjoy her one cigarette. But that wasn't the only reason she averted her gaze. Every time she glanced up and made eye contact with him, she felt an intensity that she'd never felt before. It was better to look away and play it cool. As cool as she could with black Cover-Girl mascara smeared all over her cheeks like some sad, pathetic clown.

"I'm sorry. Y'know, when I first found out, it was a bigger thing for me too. I just forget."

Huh? What was he talking about? Oh yeah, being adopted. *Whatever, Hot Guy. Keep trying.* She touched the cigarette to her lips and inhaled.

The guy stood there for a moment, gazing at her. She could tell he was trying to find a way to turn the conversation around. "Listen, I was about to grab some beers and chill a little. You like beer?"

Beer? *Uh, yeah,* she thought. What better way to forget about everything that had happened than to chug a beer? Candace studied Hot Guy's face, unsure. He raised an eyebrow.

"I said I'm sorry. Thought maybe you could use the distraction. We're having a little get-together at my place." Some booze, new people, maybe Hot Guy was right. The distraction sounded nice.

"I could use a beer."

"What kind?" he asked, a little more at ease.

"Doesn't matter." The truth was, Candace didn't know much about beer. She'd drank it a few times before, mostly at parties, but it usually came in a keg and she had no idea what the name of it was. She'd also snuck a beer once from the unattended cooler at a barbeque her mom dragged her to, but it was thick and foamy and dark-colored, and it tasted so bitter Candace couldn't even finish it. She hoped he didn't get that kind.

Smiling, the beautiful boy reached into the pocket of his faded jeans and pulled out his wallet. "I'll be right back." As he entered the store, Candace watched him through the window, exhaling a thin stream of smoke.

As Candace watched Hot Guy stroll over to the illuminated cooler where the cases of beer were displayed, she realized he could see her peeking in at him through the reflection in the glass door, and quickly turned away from the window. Embarrassed, Candace stubbed the cigarette butt out in an ashtray filled with dirty sand. She pulled a tube of Passion Pink gloss from her purse, and spread it across her lips with expert precision. Then she glanced, more carefully this time, in the window and saw the clerk accepting cash from the adopted hot guy and handing him a brown paper bag. As Hot Guy turned toward the window to exit the store, Candace put on her best disinterested face.

"Act like you don't care what they do," Candace had advised Avery on more than one occasion. "They'll think you're more intriguing and mysterious that way." Avery never listened, though. It embarrassed Candace to watch her best friend follow around the guys she was crushing on like some pathetic little puppy.

"How am I supposed to start a conversation with him if I'm not standing close enough to hear what he's saying?" Avery had said at the last party they went to. It was the same party that Avery's current love interest, Pablo, showed up to wearing old-school Vans and board shorts under a ripped tank top. Pablo had just moved to LA from San Juan, Puerto Rico, and he had an incredible accent that made everything he said sound profound and sexy. Half of the girls at their high school were in love with him and most were playing it a thousand times cooler than Avery.

"You don't," Candace explained as they peeked over

at Pablo standing in the corner. "Just laugh and act like you're having a better time over here and you don't even notice him and it'll make him wish he was part of our conversation." Avery couldn't pull it off, though. Pablo kept catching her looking over at him and her laughs sounded incredibly fake. Candace finally gave up and told Avery that if she really wanted to go orbit around him like a weirdo, she should just do it. Avery did. And of course, she didn't end up in any sort of meaningful conversation with Pablo.

Candace knew better. She knew how to get guys interested. Keeping them more into her than sophomore volleyball players, well, that was a different story.

As the hot stranger sidled up next to her, he pulled a tacky chocolate rose wrapped in red foil from the paper bag. There was a green plastic stem attached complete with two plastic leaves, one of which curled up unnaturally. He handed the Frankenstein of a flower to her.

"For you, little orphan Annie. Someone told me that women love roses and chocolate." There was a gleam in his eye as he said it, oozing with confidence.

"Which one is this?" Candace quipped, trying to be funny. It was, after all, a sad amalgamation of both. Unfortunately, her choice of words made her appear completely ungrateful.

"Fine," he said, sounding a little offended as he plucked it out of her hand. "I'll eat it myself."

"Hold up there, Romeo." She playfully snatched it back. Now it was Candace trying to turn the conversation around. She had no idea that under his tough, rugged exterior, this guy was actually quite sensitive. "I didn't say I didn't want it."

"Romeo?" He raised an eyebrow. The chemistry was real and they could both feel it. He pulled a bottle of vodka from the bag.

"Someone also told me women like vodka. . . ."

"This one does," Candace responded, pleased with his choice. She reached for the bottle, ready to twist off the cap, but the guy pulled it away.

"Not in public," he warned, and then made a motion for her to follow him to his pickup truck. As he walked off ahead of her, she hurried to catch up. *Maybe*, she thought, *this day is going to end a lot better than it started. . . .*

FOUR
CROSSING THE TRACKS

Hot Guy's truck cruised down La Cienega Boulevard, dipping in and out of the glow of streetlights. They were on the way back to his house. Candace sat in front, sipping from the vodka bottle. The barred store windows and abandoned furniture in the alleys made her question whether she should've left her car parked at the gas station. *I'm sure it's fine*, she thought, sure she'd locked it. Tonight wasn't about being responsible. It was about forgetting her problems, and stressing over whether someone would break in and steal the change out of the ashtray wasn't on the agenda.

Candace was semi-aware that Hot Guy's gaze was lingering on her thighs. She didn't mind. After all, he was a guy, and guys look. Swallowing the burn, she wiped her mouth with the sleeve of her jacket and screwed the cap back.

"Wow." She coughed. "That's . . . strong."

He smiled. "Feeling a little better?"

Candace nodded. Hot Guy was a nice distraction from all the heavy thoughts and confusion that had plagued her mind a half hour earlier. She was already thinking about the question she wanted to ask him. "So . . . how did you find out you were adopted?"

Without taking his eyes off the road, he shrugged and launched into the mini version of his life as if it were no more important than describing what he'd had for dinner.

"It wasn't like I didn't know. My whole childhood I got bounced around as different family members took care of me. I lived with my grandma and then my aunt . . . and then my other aunt. Finally, I went into a foster home and stayed there till I was, like, eighteen. Then I left."

"You left?" she inquired, as if trying to figure out how she could pull off the same escape.

"Well, yeah," he said, as if it were obvious. "Once you're eighteen, they gotta kick you out of the system. I guess I wasn't technically adopted by anyone."

"Where were your mom and dad?"

"Never had a dad. My mom wasn't allowed to keep me. Social Services wouldn't let her."

"Why not?" Candace asked as she took another sip from the bottle.

"Lots of reasons. She never shoulda had a kid is probably the number one."

She waited for him to say more but he didn't. Just kept driving.

"That's a sad story," Candace said, genuinely meaning it. She looked over at him, checking to see if he was upset, but he didn't seem bothered. Instead he grinned.

"I'm not the one with mascara all streaked down my face, though, am I?"

Candace knew he was poking fun at her, but had to smile just a little.

"So what's your story?" he asked.

Candace looked back out the window. "Well, apparently I was born to parents I've never met." Musing over this, she added, "I guess it makes sense now why I never get along with my mom. She's not even my real mother."

"How 'bout your dad?"

"They got divorced about two years ago. He lives kinda far away so we only see him on holidays and school breaks."

"We?"

"My brother, Andrew, and me. I guess I shouldn't call him that. He's not my real brother," she said, suddenly a little more down than she was a moment ago. Hot Guy chuckled. She looked over at him curiously.

"You sure do a good job feeling sorry for yourself."

She gave him an admonishing look. "Don't be a dick."

He laughed and turned his focus back to the road.

Pulling up to Hot Guy's house, it looked like there was a party going on inside. The music emanated through the open windows, a backing track to the strains of drunken laughter and people trying to talk over one another.

"Busy place," Candace commented as she hopped out of his truck. She looked around, a little surprised that no one on the block seemed to mind the noise. In her neighborhood, this kind of party would've been shut down before it ever started. She glanced up at the buzzing streetlight that flickered sporadically on the other side of the road—not broken, but on the cusp of giving up. *Just like this neighborhood*, she thought. Candace could tell her thoughts were coming slow. She was starting to feel the effects of the alcohol and stumbled slightly as she made her way up the uneven pavers. Halfway to the front door, Candace jumped when the neighbor's dog charged out of the darkness and barked as it lunged into the six-foot-high metal fence. Hot Guy laughed and took her arm to steady her.

"That dog hates me," he said as he opened the door. Holding her hand in his, he led her quickly through the living room filled with old, mismatched furniture and a new flat-screen television that was muted but on. The place was packed with people laughing and drinking beer and passing around a bong. Candace noted that it was a mixed crowd—some of the characters looked a lot like her own friends, only a few years older. There were a couple of guys and one lady in particular who seemed a *lot* older. Almost as old as Candace's parents, but nothing like her parents. One of the guys was wearing a leather vest with a motorcycle gang logo on it. The woman had her nose, lip, and eyebrow pierced. As they passed by the kitchen, Candace could see them playing cards and doing shots. Moving through the crowd, a few people acknowledged them, sizing her up.

"Hey, Toby," a dark-haired, tattooed girl in a crop top said, smiling somewhat pleasantly until she noticed him tugging Candace along behind. Then the girl shook her head, annoyed, and turned her back to them. *Hot Guy has a name*, Candace thought, barely able to keep the realization in her head long enough to process it. Toby. Toby, Toby, Toby. She repeated in her brain, hoping she wouldn't forget.

Heading down the narrow hallway, the skunky stench of pot grew stronger. Halfway to the back of the house, they passed an open door to a small bedroom. Although she only got a brief look, she could see a guy sitting on the edge of a bed while a really skinny girl with bleached-blond hair in a Betty Page cut gave him a lap dance in her bra and panties. Candace didn't realize she'd stopped walking and was staring at the guy until he looked directly at her. Without taking his gaze off Candace, he planted his palms firmly on the ass of the girl who was bent over in front of him. Then he nodded for Candace to join them. She quickly moved on and caught up with Toby, who was using a key to unlock a door at the end of the hall.

Toby entered his room and went right to a makeshift

bar that doubled as a dresser. Candace lingered in the doorway, gazing around at the old furnishings and tattered posters of bands she'd never heard of hanging on the wall.

"Shut that," he instructed her.

She closed the door, giving them some quiet from the music and privacy from the mayhem going on in the front of the house. Toby pulled the vodka bottle out and poured some into two glasses. As she watched him take a swig off the bottle before screwing the cap back on, Candace began to wonder what she'd gotten herself into. Here she was, half-inebriated, in the room of a guy she'd just met. Anything could happen. In her earlier emotional state, she clearly hadn't thought this plan through. *If Mom ever found out I got into a car with a guy I met at a gas station and didn't even know his name, she'd kill me,* Candace thought.

Then: *Wait, no. I have to stop calling her that. She's not my mom. Why would she even care what I do?*

She gazed at her new friend. Toby. *Hopefully this guy doesn't murder me. He's too gorgeous to be a serial killer, right?*

When Candace took an awkward step back toward the door, Toby nodded to the bed.

"You can sit," he said.

Candace hesitated and feigned interest in one of his Sex Pistols posters as she perched on the edge of his king-size bed. If he suddenly pulled out a machete or something, she was pretty sure she could make it out the door and down the hall where if he were going to hack her up, at least she'd have witnesses.

She mused to herself. *Okay, now I'm really being weird. Go back to the aloof, mysterious Candy everyone knows and few people love.* As he handed her a glass, he said through a toothy grin, "Vodka cures everything."

Candace couldn't get past the thoughts of being murdered. "I should probably go," she said, standing back up nervously.

Toby seemed baffled. "Go where? Back to your mom's house?"

She shrugged.

"We just got here," he said. "Let's put some music on and just chill."

As he walked over to his sound system and started scrolling through playlists, she took a cautious sip of her drink. He glanced back at her a few times with an odd look, so she forced a tense smile.

"What are you worried about?" he asked, somewhat

offended. "You act like I'm going to rape you or something."

Candace, a little embarrassed, picked at a loose thread on his bedspread.

"That's funny because I was just wondering that very thing," she said, trying to make light of the situation. Toby couldn't help but smile at her comment. His eyes sparkled as he sat down beside her and put a finger under her chin, lifting her face to look at him.

"Hey," he said with sincerity. "I brought you here because I like you. And I wanna cheer you up. Nothing's gonna happen if you don't want it to, okay?"

She nodded, feeling a little more at ease.

"Trust me. I don't need to force myself on anyone."

Did he really have to say that? For a moment she felt jealousy rise up inside her. Not in the über-intense, fiery way she did when she saw Ian and Jenny sucking face in the hallway outside the Spanish room, but still, she didn't need to picture girls popping off their bras and panties and climbing on top of this guy. After all, she was starting to like him a little.

"That's a very convincing argument," she said, letting go of her paranoia. "I'm pretty sure Ted Bundy used that exact argument in court." She waited to see if he knew who Ted Bundy was.

Toby let out a laugh. "You're funny," he said. "Maybe I'm the one that should be worried . . . bringing a random girl into my room and I don't even know her name."

"Candace," she replied, lightening up a little. "But everyone calls me Candy."

"Well, Candy, I'm Toby. And now that we got that out of the way, are you more in the mood for reggae? Or industrial metal?"

Candace took a sip of her vodka and smiled. "I think it's more of a reggae night."

"I couldn't agree more."

FIVE
GOOD GIRLS AND VERY BAD BOYS

Candace was so busy scrolling through her phone for a photo of Avery, she barely noticed Toby grabbing the bottle and pouring a little more booze into her glass.

"I really want to find this one picture," she slurred. As she swiped each photo off the screen, she realized that most of the pictures she had also featured Avery. Seeing the goofy shots that she should have deleted long ago made Candace smile.

"She's such a good person," Candace remarked as she studied a photo of the two of them at the beach. They'd traded bikini tops so they were each wearing the same mismatched swimsuits but conversely. "And such a great friend. I've known her for, like, years and years. Who knows? Maybe we even knew each other in a previous life." Candace giggled as she took another sip of her newly filled glass.

"If she's your bestie and all that, why did you send her call to voice mail?" Toby asked, parting his lips slightly. In her inebriated state, Candace had already forgotten that the whole reason she even picked up her phone was because it had started ringing. Avery had been calling and yes, as Toby pointed out, she had indeed sent the call to voice mail.

"Here it is!" Candace said, ignoring his question, and turned the phone around. It was a photo of her and Avery acting goofy at a high school basketball game. They'd painted the school's mascot—a bull—on their cheeks. After sweating in a hot gymnasium for a couple of hours, the bull was hardly recognizable. It looked more like a brown blob with horns. Candace knew when Toby squinted and then enlarged the image that he was trying to figure out what it was.

"That's Buddy the Bull," Candace explained. "Our mascot. It looked better at the beginning of the game."

"Looks more like bull*shit*." Toby chuckled and

handed the phone back to her. Candace grinned, knowing he was right. It did sort of look like someone had smeared a cow turd on their skin.

"So why are you avoiding Avery's calls?" he asked, before throwing back his own shot of booze.

"Because . . ." Candace began. "I'm sure my mom's called her by now and she's gonna try to talk me into going home. I know she will because she's always super-levelheaded and stuff." Candace's voice drifted off as she drunkenly searched for more photos, a sense of loss coming over her. Avery was the only part of her past that she wanted to keep: she was the only person Candy could trust. What would Avery say when she told her that she was dropping out of school and never going back? Probably that she was having an irrational moment and needed to sleep it off. *I'm not irrational, though*, Candace thought. *Why would I want to stay in a place where everyone lies to me? Where I don't fit in? There are so many better things out there. So many things that my parents didn't want me to know. Sometimes you just have to see where you end up. Like tonight, if I hadn't bailed out of there and gone into that gas station, I never would've met the excessively yummy guy sitting across from me. I never would have ended up back here at his house, listening to Jamaican drums, drinking vodka, and forgetting about my crap ball of a week.*

Avery's the only one I can trust. But I can call her back tomorrow.

Toby gazed at her as she drunkenly searched for more photos. There was an innocence to her pictures that he found enticing. *She* was enticing. And beautiful. He liked how she kept pushing her hair out of her face as she cocked her head to the side, looking at her phone. The hair would fall, she'd push it back, only to have it fall again. Where the hell did this girl come from? It was as if someone plucked her out of a PG-rated movie about a place where all the houses were surrounded by white picket fences and kids could play in the street, and dropped her into an R-rated film where every character has an angle and it can be hard to tell the good guys from the bad.

Goddamn, her life at seventeen is so different than mine was, he thought as he switched playlists to one with some old nineties tracks. By that age, he'd been kicked out of high school and was going half days to an alternative school in Van Nuys. He could still remember watching his aunt make his brown-bag lunch as he tried to convince her to let him skip his first day of school.

"Toby, you've got to go to school, kiddo," his aunt

Patricia had said as she overspread a glob of mayonnaise on a piece of bologna.

"What are you so worried about?" she asked, unwrapping a slice of American cheese. As she dropped it onto his sandwich, her short reddish-brown hair fell over her dark eyes and she blew a quick puff of air from her lips, sending it back out of her round, pudgy face.

"Nothing," Toby had lied as he chewed on his dirty fingernail. He was worried about everything. This was his fourth school in five years and he was pretty sure that like all the other schools, the teachers would hate him. He didn't want to be living with Patricia again. He liked that his mother's sister wasn't on drugs the way his own mom was, but if he had the choice he would have stayed with his grandma. He didn't care what the stupid courts said. She wasn't too sick to take care of him.

Patricia smiled and foraged through the refrigerator looking for something additional to add to the two lunches she was packing. "Don't stress your little head about nothing," she assured him. "If anyone bothers you, Keenan will be all over their asses."

As if on cue when Patricia mentioned his name, Keenan walked into the room. "I can hear you talking about me," he said with more confidence than most thirteen-year-olds.

"Oh relax," Patricia muttered with mild amusement. "Ain't sayin' nothing bad. Keep your cousin outta trouble today, you hear me?"

Keenan glanced over at Toby as he picked up an apple and spun it around on the table.

"By the way, Hank told Gage he couldn't smoke in the house."

Toby watched silently for Patricia's reaction as the spinning apple came to a stop.

"Pot?" she asked.

"No, Mom. Cigarettes." Keenan reached for the apple to spin it again but Toby quickly pulled it away, grinning. Keenan smiled too and flopped over the table, grabbing Toby's arm.

"If Gage has a problem with Hank, he can talk to me about it. Don't be starting shit between your brothers and your stepfather."

"I'm not starting anything. I'm just filling you in on what I witnessed," Keenan protested, pulling the apple from Toby's weaker grip and making a point of biting into it. Toby silently laughed as Keenan made a show of chewing the mashed-up apple with his mouth open, letting pieces of pulpy red skin fall out and onto his shirt.

Toby didn't like Patricia's boyfriend, Hank. He was always harassing one of her older sons about one thing or another. And when she wasn't around, which was a lot of the time, he'd start trouble with Keenan, too.

That's another reason Toby wished he could stay with his grandma. She didn't like Hank either. Ever since Patricia had shown up on Saturday morning wearing cheap sunglasses to cover a bruise on her cheek, Hank had been banned from Grandma's house. Toby was pretty sure that Hank was unaware of his blacklist status.

"Hank's an ass," Keenan had said to Toby one night as they were lying on the floor playing blackjack.

"Why doesn't your mom kick him out?" Toby asked. It was something he'd been wondering for a long time and he'd heard his grandma have conversations with Patricia about it when he was still living with her.

"She said cuz she works so much so she doesn't have time to find anyone else."

"She should meet someone at the motel," Toby said, offering the best relationship advice a ten-year-old could.

"Dummy, she's a maid. How can she meet some-one when there's no one in the room? By the time she gets there, all the people are already gone. Plus there's all truckers at that motel. She said she doesn't like 'em because they all screw hookers."

Toby wasn't sure what Keenan meant by that but it made him think about his own mom. The day the people from CPS came with his grandmother and took him away, a pretty lady in a suit had asked him where his mother was.

"She's at a motel," he said. At least he thought she was. That's where his mother said she was going two days earlier when she left him with a brand-new box of Cap'n Crunch cereal and a bag of gummy worms. Toby had liked it when his mom would go to motels because she always came back with money to buy stuff. This time, however, his mom hadn't come home that evening and Toby stayed up watching late-night TV shows, waiting for her to come back. When the cereal ran out the next day and the candy was gone, he started to get worried so he called his grandma. When she arrived, she brought the CPS people with her.

"Does Hank screw hookers?" Toby asked as he drew a new card from the deck and shoved his hand into a bowl of potato chips Patricia had brought in for them.

"Hank's too lazy to do anything," Keenan said without emotion. "Except try to beat me up." The truth was, Hank was especially hard on Keenan and it wasn't unusual for their fights to get physical.

"If he beats you up, he's gonna have to beat me up too," Toby assured him, feeling some solidarity with his cousin. Keenan was the closest thing Toby had ever had to a brother and he didn't want to see him get hurt.

"Shit," Keenan said without looking up. "He will anyway. You got twenty-one, by the way."

We couldn't be more different, Toby thought as he stared at Candace's perfectly smooth skin and the delicate gold bracelet that hung from her wrist. He pictured what her life must've been like when she woke up this morning. Probably in some big, comfy bed with cushy pillows from one of those expensive home goods stores in the mall where a set of sheets costs a hundred bucks or more. Her mom probably makes breakfast every morning and asks her if she wants juice with her coffee that comes from a machine where you use pods to make one cup at a time. Most people he knew would think she's a spoiled brat, he thought. But Toby felt like he could see beyond all that. Inside her picture-perfect exterior was a girl who was trapped in a life she didn't want, as comfortable as it was. She was surrounded by pretty things but also all kinds of ugliness and she was looking for something different. In his heart, Toby had been looking for something different, too.

Ian's goofy smile stared up at Candace, who made a gagging noise as she handed the phone to Toby. Seeing his face still sent hot barbs through Candace's stomach.

"That's him," she said as Toby held up the vodka bottle. She shook her head no. Candace still had a few swallows left in her glass, but she'd given up on trying to finish her drink. She didn't want to get sick and one more drink would've put her over the edge. Getting wasted to the point of throwing up was not the way to impress a guy. No amount of mints can fix vomit breath. Gross. Toby poured one for himself as he turned his attention to her phone. She watched him study the picture, wondering if he would feel even a little bit jealous of Ian. Instead he just scoffed.

"You are *way* too hot for this guy. What were you thinking?"

She grinned at the compliment and leaned in sloppily. As she moved, the booze in her glass sloshed around precariously, so Toby took it from her hand and set it on the nightstand.

"You think I'm hot?" she said, teasing him.

"I think you're very hot," he said. "And I think you can do better than some skinny high school jock." He pressed his face closer to hers.

"Do you have someone specific in mind?" she said, stumbling a little over the words.

Toby laughed. "I might."

"Show me what ya got," she said. Any inhibitions she had earlier were long gone. Toby stood and peeled off his T-shirt, revealing the top half of a perfectly ridged body. Not an ounce of fat covered his toned abs and thick chest.

Holy crap, Candace thought as she took in his strong arms and wide shoulders. Ian had a nice build, but he was only seventeen. Toby, on the other hand, looked like a *man*. Candace, who had felt sassy and in control moments before, found herself awkwardly quiet. Toby knelt down beside her.

"Do I pass?"

Candace nodded slowly, unable to take her eyes off the tattoo that covered Toby's left pec. It was a demon beheading a grim reaper, and it gave her something to look at rather than letting her gaze rove back and forth over his naked torso.

Toby smiled and leaned in. He paused momentarily to see if she'd move back. When she didn't, he kissed her gently on the lips at first, then harder. He slid his tongue into her mouth and within seconds, they'd fallen back onto his bed, where he pulled her on top of him and they continued to kiss.

This is what a kiss is supposed to be like, Candace thought as she pressed her palms against the inside of Toby's hard biceps. There was no slobber, no dying-fish flapping; just Toby's perfect tongue, which barely slid between her lips before retreating back into his perfect mouth.

It didn't take long before the drunken haze that had overtaken Candace's state of mind affected her body, too. As she let her hands glide down his smooth chest to the top of his jeans, she started to feel the room spinning. Before she knew it, nausea set in and she was scared she was going to be sick. Candace rolled off Toby and stared up at the ceiling.

"You okay?" he asked.

"I drank too much," she said tightly, trying to stay as still as possible.

"Are you gonna puke?" She could hear the alarm in his voice.

"I don't know. Don't say 'puke.' It makes it worse."

Why is this happening to me? She silently seethed at the universe. Finally, she had a chance to make out with one of the sexiest guys she'd ever met and her stupid stomach had other ideas? Was life just a series of cruel jokes? Why didn't she stop drinking sooner?

Toby stood up. "I'll get you some water," he said, and walked out of the room. Candace closed her eyes and tried to imagine a cool sea breeze blowing against her face. Her mother had taught her that when she was a little girl and had become sick with the flu.

"Imagine a cool burst of air rolling off the ocean and hitting you right in the cheeks," her mom had said as Candace lay on the sofa, an empty trash can standing by. The imagery helped keep her mind of the awful nauseated feeling in her gut. Candace tried to visualize the crashing waves and a mist of sea spray. But that's as far as she got. Candace passed out.

Toby hurried down the hall and poked his head through the open bedroom door. The girl that was giving the lap dance earlier was now asleep under the sheets, and the guy who had been enjoying it was taking a hit off a small water bong.

"Keenan!" Toby said as he passed his cousin, grabbed the little white plastic trash can in the corner, and yanked the garbage out of it. "I need this!" Dropping the garbage bag on the floor, he caught a glimpse of Keenan's shrug as he raced out the door. He could still hear the gurgle of the bong rip all the way into the living room.

As Toby slid into the kitchen, he practically pushed partygoers out of the way in an effort to throw open the cupboard. There were no clean glasses. Only a chipped coffee mug that would have to do.

As he filled the mug with tap water, Keenan's friend Pedro leaned against the counter next to him, a compact mirror in his hand. "Gray hair already. Can you believe that?" Pedro, who had never been particularly vain or interested in his appearance, ruffled his fingers over the crown of his hair, trying to show Toby the gray.

"That's what a hard life does to you," Toby joked back.

"That's what *kids* do to you, man. You start worrying about shit you never worried about before." Toby chuckled. He knew Pedro was kidding. Pedro loved his little daughter and proudly showed pictures of her to anyone who would look. "Seriously though, no one told me I'd be gray by twenty-eight. That's early, right?"

"You tell me, old man." Toby smirked and adjusted the faucet to make the water colder.

"Where's your cousin?" Pedro asked in his low, guttural voice.

"In his bedroom," Toby said, feeling the water and grimacing that it was still too warm. He dumped the water out and started to refill the cup.

"Did he talk to you yet about the opportunity?"

"Huh?" Toby was only half listening. "No."

"He will. Listen to what he has to say," Pedro instructed, a sly smile on his hardened face.

"Sure," Toby uttered before shutting off the faucet and hurrying back into the hall. He was on a mission to get Candace everything she needed before she spewed vomit all over his bedroom. Besides that, he wasn't too interested in what Pedro wanted to discuss. Although Pedro was cordial, Toby didn't like him much. Pedro and Keenan became friends when they met up in County after Keenan had been arrested for, according to him, "being at the wrong place at the wrong time," and Pedro was serving sixty days on a battery charge.

Apart, trouble seemed to follow each of them around. It was triple when they were together.

When Toby reached the bedroom with the trash can and the water, Keenan was already standing just inside the door ogling Candace, who had passed out on the bed. Toby didn't like the way his cousin's eyes didn't move from her slightly parted thighs and the mini skirt that had inadvertently worked its way up her hips. He stepped protectively between his cousin and Candace, facing Keenan.

Keenan instinctively stepped back.

"Nice job, man," Keenan said, keeping his voice at a whisper. "She's hot as hell."

Toby set down the water and trash can. "What's up?" he asked.

"I gotta talk to you about something Pedro told me tonight."

"Not now. Later."

"Dude, it's *big*."

"I'm interested. Just not right now." Toby nodded to the door, wanting Keenan to leave them alone. "Beat it."

Keenan, irritated, walked out. Toby looked down at Candace and gently pulled a few strands of hair from her face. Then he climbed into bed next to her and softly caressed her smooth cheek.

Man, this girl is just beautiful, he thought. It was no secret how much she turned him on. He wished she hadn't passed out, but he certainly wasn't going to try anything the way Keenan would have. He wasn't that type. Toby saw himself as a pretty decent guy and tonight, he was going to prove it. He'd made a promise to Candace that nothing would happen, and he intended to keep that promise. She'd had a rough week and he was determined to make it at least a little better.

Rolling over, his mind drifted to Keenan. He wondered what Pedro and his cousin wanted to "talk to him" about. It was most likely something illegal and dangerous. Those two liked big risks and big rewards. Not Toby. Sure, he'd done some bad stuff in his twenty-three years, but nothing like that. Nothing where someone could physically get hurt—just petty scams, check kiting, that type of low-level stuff. The few felonies he'd committed were only considered so because of the value of the items he'd stolen: expensive motorcycles and bikes, a couple of cars.

He propped his head up on his arm and studied Candace's peaceful features. He wondered what tomorrow would bring for this little runaway with a fiery personality and sarcastic wit. Probably nothing. She'd probably decide that one night on the other side of the tracks was enough and go back home to the sleepy suburbs where kids with brand-new bikes rode down the picket-fence-lined streets. And he'd probably never see her again.

Oh well. Toby sighed to himself. He couldn't blame her. But that was tomorrow. Tonight, she was here with him. He couldn't give her much but he could prove to her that sometimes the world, or at least a stranger, could be kind.

With that thought lingering in his mind, Toby put an arm around Candace's waist, pulled her tightly against his chest, and fell asleep.

SIX
THE MORNING AFTER

Candace felt a gentle tug on her foot and opened her eyes to see Toby, shirtless, standing at the foot of the bed. His toned abs disappeared into the waist of faded, fraying pajama pants and he was holding a glass that had some type of thick red liquid in it.

"Good morning, beautiful," he said.

She looked up at him, confused for a moment before it registered where she was. She instantly sat up, looking down to see if she was still wearing her clothes.

"Don't worry," he said, a little hurt. "I told you nothing would happen. Are you hungover?"

Candace nodded. Hungover was an understatement. Her head was pounding and she'd never been so thirsty in her life. It was a miserable feeling.

"Very," she managed to utter, realizing she also had a sore throat.

"Here," he said, handing her the strange red concoction. "Drink this. It'll help your head."

"What's in it?" she asked as she skeptically sniffed it. It smelled like tomato juice, but looked a little paler.

"We call it a red bud. Beer and tomato juice. Trust me. It works." Figuring she couldn't feel any worse than she already did, Candace took the drink and sipped it. Toby grabbed a T-shirt off a folded pile on the floor and slipped it on.

"What time does your school start?"

"I told you I'm not going back there," she said, drinking more of the tomato stuff. It wasn't as bad as she'd anticipated. When she had run out of her house yesterday, the only thing she'd been thinking about was how she wanted to get as far away from her mother as possible. But now, lying in Toby's bed, it occurred to her that she didn't have to follow any of her mother's rules. She didn't have to go home and she certainly didn't have to go to school and deal with all the stares and whispers. She and her mother had been fighting so much the past few months, it was a relief to be away from the constant nagging.

"So now you're a dropout?" he said, half chiding her.

"Pretty much." The sassy, defiant Candace was back.

"That's a new record for being a bad influence. You've known me less than twenty-four hours." Toby grabbed her cell phone from the nightstand and handed it to her. "Your mom's been blowing up your phone all night. I had to turn the thing off."

"Good. Let her worry."

Toby shook his head with an amused look. While he grabbed deodorant from the dresser and shoved his hand up under his shirt, Candace reached down and with one finger, hooked a pack of cigarettes from the floor. Pulling one out, she popped it into her mouth.

Toby reached over and plucked it from her lips.

"Kiss me first."

Grinning, Candace leaned in and planted a long, soft kiss on Toby's mouth, her hands on each side of his face. Then she sat back and raised an eyebrow.

"That was more enthusiastic than I expected," he said, smiling.

"I'm full of surprises," she said with a glimmer.

Toby stuffed the cigarette back into the pack.

"Today is the day you quit smoking, by the way."

"Says who?" Candace asked, surprised.

"Says me. You're too pretty to smoke."

Candace softened a little, appreciating the compliment. She was fairly sure the sore throat she had was from yesterday's cigarette, and since she could count on one hand the number of times she'd ever had a cigarette anyway, she figured she'd give him an easy win.

"And you're too bossy. But I don't mind," she said flirtatiously.

Toby grinned. "So . . . if you're not going to school today and you're not going home . . . what's your plan?"

"Can I hang out here? I'm sure you and I could find *something* to do. . . ." She kissed him again. The truth was, the more time she spent with Toby, the more she liked him. And she wanted a chance to get to know him better, see what it was like to live life in this world. It had to be better than the one she came from.

He studied her for a moment, then stood up. "Okay. How about I take you out for breakfast, we go get your car, and then we can come back here and have a little fun . . . ?"

Candace smiled, liking the agenda. "I say yes."

Thirty minutes later, Toby and Candace were sitting in a booth of a little breakfast joint, eating omelets. Toby stuffed a bite into his mouth and then picked up his phone to respond to a text. Candace observed him, intrigued.

Eating breakfast in a restaurant on a school day made her feel like an adult with freedom. For the first time ever, Candace felt like she had choices. No one was telling her she had to sit through some lame class and listen to some godawful lecture about things that didn't matter. Adults get to decide what they're going to do each day, and today, like all the other people sitting in Gabby's Diner, *she'd* decided—to skip school and order a Denver omelet, side of fruit salad, and a cup of coffee.

"Fun playing hooky, isn't it?" she asked as she popped a grape into her mouth.

"I guess," he responded without looking up. "I'm working as we sit here."

"What do you mean? What do you do?" Whatever his job was, she wanted it.

"I'm a businessman." He squinted at the phone, waiting for the next text to come in.

That wasn't the answer she was expecting. Avery's dad was a businessman and he was stuck in an office ten hours a day. Evidently, Avery's dad had picked the wrong business.

"Could you be more . . . vague?" she asked, making fun of him a little. He finally looked up at her, wiping his mouth with the paper napkin that had once been rolled around his fork and knife.

"I loan people money when a bank won't give 'em loans."

Candace pursed her lips. "You mean like a loan shark?" she asked.

Toby chuckled.

"No, silly. It's called P2P lending. There's risk involved but the returns are good."

Candace contemplated this for a moment as she picked up a strip of bacon and crunched off the end. She'd never heard of P2P lending but it sounded official and interesting.

"Do you make a lot of money?"

Toby studied her with a smile. "Why? You want me to buy you something already?"

"Nooooo," she said, laughing. "Just breakfast." He'd better buy her breakfast because all she had in her purse was the same seven dollars and change from the night before.

Toby grinned. "Is the interrogation over with? Or are we just on a break?" he inquired.

"Nothing wrong with getting to know you better, right?" she said in a light tone, but in all honestly, she was serious. He intrigued her.

"Nothing wrong with getting to me know me better, huh?" Toby repeated, and arched an eyebrow as if he wasn't quite sure he agreed. Then, changing his mind, he put the cell phone down.

"Okay. There's somethin' *I'd* like to ask." He looked her square in the face.

"Go ahead. Unlike you, I'm an open book." She punctuated the last part by taking a bite of her apple wedge.

"You said last night you hated your mom. Why?"

Candace became more reserved, her mood darkening.

The last thing she wanted to think about right now was her mom and her adoptive status.

"I don't remember saying that."

"You talk a lot when you're drunk." He smiled, but she didn't. What else had she said? Hopefully nothing embarrassing. Unfortunately, she'd just insisted that she was an open book so she felt compelled to answer his question. Even though his curiosity made her uncomfortable, she liked that he was interested in her answer.

"She's a pain in the ass and that's why my dad left," she said quickly.

"Where's he live?" Toby asked, shoving a bite of hash browns into his mouth. "You mentioned he lived kinda far away."

"San Diego. I don't get to see him that much. I didn't really get to see him a lot before, though. He's an airline pilot so he's gone all the time."

"Is that why your mom's a pain? She complained about him being gone?" Toby's follow-up question made sense but it wasn't just that her mom complained. She did—often—but it was more complicated than that. She was a pain in so many ways.

"Yes," Candace explained. "But also we just don't get along. All she cares about is me going to college, and I don't even know if I want to go to college. Plus, she flips out on me constantly."

Toby seemed somewhat relieved by her answer. Candace wasn't sure why.

"College isn't for everyone," he said matter-of-factly.

Finally! she thought. *Someone who agrees with me!*

"It's definitely not for me. I can't imagine sitting in a classroom for four more years. That's like a prison sentence. Except you can't get out early for good behavior." Toby laughed and nearly choked on his coffee. She grinned, not realizing she'd said anything funny. She was just being herself.

"I have never met anyone quite like you," he mused as he set his cup down.

"And you never will," she said with a smile.

From the look on his face, she knew he agreed.

Outside of the gas station, Toby's pickup slowed to a stop next to Candace's car—still parked, safe and sound, where she'd left it the night before.

"And . . . we're back to the beginning," he said. "You want to follow me to my place or just GPS it?"

"I doubt I have enough gas to make it," she said, and started to fish some cash from the bottom of her purse. Toby smiled and pulled out a twenty.

"I got it. Just pull up to the pump."

Candace sat behind the wheel and watched as Toby put gas in her tank, just like her father used to do for her mother when they were married. When the meter hit twenty, he stuffed the nozzle back in place and leaned down near her window. Candace smiled.

"I'm actually going to run home and grab a change of clothes before I come over, okay? My mom's at work so I can sneak in and sneak out without anyone noticing." Candace felt gross wearing the same outfit she had on the entire day before. Plus, she'd slept in it. Even grosser. She wasn't sure how long she'd be staying at Toby's but she figured she'd hang out as long as he'd let her. He didn't seem to want her to go anytime soon.

"Will they be sexy clothes?" he asked.

"Maybe . . ." she said evasively. She liked how he flirted with her. And she also liked that he didn't try to talk her out of what she said she wanted to do. If she'd told Ian she wanted to run home and get clothes, it would've turned into a twenty-minute conversation about why she should just borrow some of his clothes, or worse yet, his mother's. Toby was just so chill. He went with the flow and she liked that.

He smiled. "Gimme your phone."

She handed him the phone and he entered his address into her GPS before handing it back to her. Then he leaned in and kissed her gently on the lips.

"See ya later, gorgeous."

"Bye," she said, and noticed he wasn't driving away. Turning back, she yelled, "What are you doing?"

He rolled down the window so she could hear him.

"Being a gentleman and waiting for you to leave first."

He was being serious, and it made her laugh. She waved him off. He honked once—a friendly, lighthearted honk—and then backed up, driving off down the street. Candace watched him go. She sat there for a moment in the driver's seat, thinking about this boy she'd just met. *He's far from a boy*, she thought. *Ian is a boy. Toby is a* man. Maybe this was the kind of guy she should've been going for all along—self-sufficient, sexy, smart enough to run his own business. *He just might be everything I'm looking for*, she mused as she started her car and headed back to her mother's. But could she cut ties with her old life and start a brand-new one less than fifteen miles away? It wouldn't be easy. She was sure that by now her mother had called her father and told him about their argument, and that she hadn't come home last night. They might even be out looking for her. It didn't matter. In less than five months, she'd be eighteen and then she could do anything she wanted. She'd have complete control over her own life and there was nothing they could say or do about it. *Maybe this whole running-away thing, this finding out I'm adopted, is going to change my life for the better*, she thought. *If so, it's about time.*

SEVEN
A NEAR MISS

Candace's car pulled past the driveway of her mother's two-story house and stopped. She sat behind the wheel, staring at the white siding and dark green shutters, the autumn wreath that graced the oversize door, and the two bougainvillea bushes that flanked the front porch. Their papery pink leaves dotted the yard. How many of those pink leaves were hidden between the pages of books tucked away in her closet or the den? When she was little, she and Andrew would sift through the fallen leaves, finding the perfect ones, and then hide them in random books for their parents to find.

Candace sighed. It was all so familiar yet it didn't feel like *her* home anymore. It felt foreign—like it belonged to someone else. *It's bizarre how quickly things can change*, she thought. *Yesterday morning, I thought it was going to be a regular day at school.* There couldn't be very many times in a person's life where things changed so drastically. Getting married, graduating from high school, having a baby . . . But at least in those moments you expected your life to change. She had been totally unprepared.

She got out of the car and peeked into the garage through the window to make sure her mother's SUV wasn't there. The garage was empty, coast clear. Hurrying, she let herself in, ran up the stairs, and entered her room.

Candace took in the room that used to be hers: the puffy duvet with orange hibiscus silhouettes, the shelf with all her books and trinkets she'd collected over the years, the small oak desk where she sometimes did her homework but more often than not, simply messed around online when she was supposed to be working out equations for Precalc. Having just spent the night at Toby's, Candace noticed how stark the differences between their rooms were. Toby's room barely had anything that matched anything else: the blankets and pillowcases and sheets all seemed to have come from different places; the curtains were old and ripped; his dresser was missing a few knobs, which meant you had to pry the drawers open with your fingernails. In this room, everything matched. The pale gray curtains and the paint and the pillows and the even the throw blanket that hung lazily over the arm of the overstuffed chair in the corner. It was picture-perfect. And yet, this place couldn't feel more *imperfect*. Toby's bedroom was proof that none of it was necessary. *He has mismatched, secondhand stuff and he's perfectly happy*, she thought. *It's time for me to be happy too. It's time for me to stop living a fake life and to figure out what my purpose is on this planet. I'm going to find out who I really am, what I truly want out of life, and then I'm going to go after it like a madwoman.* With a smile on her face, she started stuffing clothes into a duffel bag.

After pulling as much as she could pack from the closet, she moved to the dresser, where she opened one of the drawers and found her sexiest bra and panty set—a cute Victorian lace number with vintage white trim. *He wants sexy*, she thought. *This is* sexxxyyyy.

Grabbing a few more pairs of underwear and some

bras as well as her brush, some makeup, and the phone charger hanging from the outlet on her wall, she shoved them into her bag and headed back down the stairs. As she reached the front door, she caught a glimpse of her mom's car pulling into the drive. Candace froze. *What the hell was she doing home?* She stood there, unable to move her feet as she watched her mother leap out of her silver SUV. From the speed with which she ran toward the house, Candace knew her mom had spotted her car parked on the street.

"Dammit!" Candace said aloud. What now?

Her only way out of the house without coming face-to-face with her mother was to slip out the back door. As quickly as the thought formed, Candace bolted down the steps and raced through the hall into the family room. She ducked behind the wall just as her mother threw open the front door.

"Candace?" her mother yelled, and immediately ascended the stairs two at a time. "Candace?!"

Candace could hear her mother's desperate cries as she carefully and quietly unlocked the patio door and slid the heavy glass to the side. The screen door was also locked. She delicately flipped the lock down, unlatching the door.

"Candace!" her mother called out again, and Candace could tell she was exiting her bedroom. In a few seconds, she'd be down the stairs searching the first floor. She needed to haul ass if she was going to get out of there.

Hearing her mother's footsteps thudding down the stairs, Candace slid open the screen door and, leaving it open, crossed the backyard, past the shed she'd helped her father build three summers ago, past the lawn darts that Andrew never put back in the bin, and pushed open the gate. Sure that her mother was only steps away from spotting her, Candace darted down the driveway and hopped into her car.

She turned the key in the ignition. Nothing but a low growl from her engine. *Don't do this to me!* she ordered as she glanced up to see her mother coming out the front door.

"Candace, stop!" her mom yelled. But Candace had no intention of stopping. She turned the key a second time and the engine roared to life. Candace yanked the transmission into drive and with squealing tires, started off down the street as her mother reached the curb.

Worried that her mother would jump into her own

vehicle and follow her, Candace glanced in the rearview mirror. She was surprised at what she saw. Instead of running toward her SUV parked in the drive, she saw her mother lower herself to the curb and hold her head in her hands. Candace's foot touched the brake and her eyes narrowed as she tried to see what her mother was doing. As her car approached the corner, her mom's image became too small to tell but Candace was pretty sure that her mother was sobbing. Right there, in front of their house, where all the neighbors could see, she was crying. A pang of guilt shot through Candace. A lump formed in her throat and her eyes began to sting. She never set out to *hurt* her mother, or anyone else. She just wanted to be left alone—to do her own thing.

She doesn't care about me anyway, Candace told herself. *If she did, she would've told me I was adopted a long time ago. She's probably crying because she loves to be in control and right now she's not.* Even as Candace tried to alleviate the heavy feeling of guilt, she knew deep down that everything she was telling herself was a lie.

Of course her mother cared about her; of course she was the reason her mom was sitting on a curb. But that just made her want to leave even more. She hated all the feelings swirling around inside her: guilt, embarrassment, regret. She'd made so many mistakes that those feelings never left her. Every time she looked at her mother, she saw the disappointment, the things she hated in herself; the things she wished she could change but just couldn't seem to get on top of.

I need this, Candace told herself. *I need to start over, totally clean, completely new, with someone like Toby who gets me. I need to find the* thing—*the thing I've been missing, even though I'm not sure what it is. I need to stop feeling like I'm failing all the time.* Her mother was the reason she felt like that. Candace knew her mom wanted her to get better grades, be more involved with her brother, choose some traditional path to success and follow it. Candace just couldn't do those things. She didn't want to. She wanted a father who still lived in the house with them and the freedom to figure out who she was. Instead, she had a mother who drove her father away, who lied, who let her make a fool of herself in front of her peers. The bottom line was that she didn't know how to stop the fighting as long as she was living under the same roof with her mom.

No! She's not my mom. She never was.

When she was around Toby those feelings were gone. She felt excitement about the future, she felt connected and grounded, she felt beautiful and mysterious. She liked how he raised his eyebrow when she talked as if he only half believed what she was saying. She liked how she'd caught him watching her in the mirror as she brushed her teeth with her finger earlier that morning. She liked how he didn't seem to let anything bother him. Here was a guy who'd had a pretty tough life, at least from what she could gather, and she was sure she hadn't even scratched the surface when it came to his past. Yet, he had bought her a silly chocolate rose after knowing her less than five minutes just to cheer her up. She liked how she felt when she was with him. And although she hated hurting her mother, it made no sense to leave the person that made her forget about her problems and go back to a place she knew she was unhappy. Eventually, her mom would have to come to that understanding as well.

"How much are we talkin'?" Toby asked as he adjusted the crate he was sitting on and watched Keenan run his finger over the VIN number on a motorcycle they'd stolen two weeks prior. It was a nice bike—a Yamaha only about a year old. Parked for several days in front of a house near the freeway on-ramp, it had been easy to load into Toby's truck in the wee hours of the morning. No one had seen a thing.

"Thirty K each," Keenan said, and let his words sink in for a moment. It was dark and cool in the garage with the door pulled down to keep potentially meddling neighbors or a patrolling cop car from catching a glimpse of what they were doing.

"Hand me that Dremel." Toby gave Keenan the small hand sander and continued to think over the grinding noise as Keenan slowly made the bike's identifying numbers disappear. Thirty thousand dollars was a lot of money, but Toby knew that kind of cash didn't come easy. For a job to net serious money, there had to be some serious risk involved. And since the plan had germinated with Pedro, risk was a given.

"All I have to do is drive?" Toby asked.

"Yep. Get us in and out fast. Pedro and I will do the dirty work." *Dirty work.* Toby didn't like the sound of that. As a matter of fact, he didn't like anything about this plan.

"How do you even know they're gonna leave the cash there by itself?" Toby asked, trying to find holes in the plan. Keenan turned off the sander and gave his cousin an incredulous look.

"Because Pedro's sources are good," Keenan retorted, as if it were the most obvious thing in the world. Toby heaved a sigh, not convinced. "Look," Keenan explained. "The best part of this whole thing is that Dawson can't go to the cops. I mean, what is he gonna say? 'Hey, Officer, I'd like to file a police report. A bunch of illegal drugs I planned to sell got ripped off'? Come on, once we're out of there, we're golden."

Toby leaned back and sipped his beer, which was starting to get warm. Dawson was known for being ruthless and vindictive. Even if they could pull off the robbery, there was a possibility that Dawson would find out who was behind it. And if he found out you were the one who screwed him over, you were as good as dead.

"I just don't get why someone as smart as Dawson would leave drugs and money unattended like that. Doesn't make sense," Toby said, trying to bring Keenan's attention back to the flaw in the logistics. From the way Keenan looked at him, Toby could tell he was frustrated with the questions.

"Because when you hide something, you think it's fucking hidden, okay? That's the point of hiding it. So you can go about your business and not sit there and guard it."

Toby rubbed the stubble on his chin. He knew if he pressed any harder, it would turn into a fight. Keenan could be explosive and the last thing Toby wanted right now was to piss his cousin off. Finally, Toby just shrugged.

"What's that supposed to mean?" Keenan asked, referring to the shrug.

"I don't know," Toby replied cautiously. "I'm doing okay with the other stuff." The truth was, Toby didn't feel like thinking about what Keenan was proposing. His mind was on Candace and whether or not she would actually come back. Toby knew there was a good chance that the time he spent with her had already come to an end. Neither had sought out the other. They'd just both been in the same place at the right time. But he'd been drawn to her immediately—her sad brown eyes and turned-up little nose that had become crimson from sniffling. Even with the gloom she carried with her, she was still a bright white blossom tucked there among a field of weeds.

He'd enjoyed the time they spent lying side by side as the party wound down in the early morning hours. He liked sitting across from her at the diner. She was a refreshing change from the other girls he knew, the ones that showed up at his parties either drunk or high. Those girls were always conniving to find ways to spend some time alone with him. One even passed him on the way to the bathroom, grabbed his arm, and slipped a wrapped condom into his hand before whispering that she was "ready anytime he was." Toby didn't blame them for liking or wanting sex. How could he? He liked it too. It wasn't that they were trying to find a way to fall into bed with him; it was more that that's *all* they seemed to want. In ten years, Toby figured those same girls—and guys for that matter—would probably be doing the same thing they did now. Going to the same parties, getting loaded every Friday and Saturday night, just to get through their zombie-like existence Monday through Friday. They had no aspirations, no dreams, nothing besides a disturbing contentment with using drugs and sex and alcohol to escape their own choices.

Candace was different. There was a depth to her that he didn't often find in other people. Candace was a lost soul searching for something meaningful. He'd been searching for the same thing. He just didn't know where he'd find it. Ironic that it would end up being at a scuzzy gas station half a mile from his house.

But maybe he'd seen her for the last time. There was a hefty chance that her parents had caught her as she tried to sneak in and pack some clothes and talked her out of returning. Or maybe she'd looked hard at her mother's bougie house and realized that there was a lot more to be said for creature comforts than she'd thought. Or maybe she'd returned all the calls of her friend—Avery, was it?—who had convinced her that running away wasn't a good idea. There were lots of variables, and although he hoped that she'd walk through the door any minute, he wouldn't put money on it.

If she didn't, he'd be disappointed for sure. But Toby also knew from experience that people come in and out of your life and most never stay. There was a solid chance that once Candace learned a little more about him and his past, she'd bolt as fast as her feet could carry her. She already knew a little about his childhood, but he'd given her the PG-rated version. There were a lot of things he'd witnessed that no one, let alone a child, ever should. By the time he was eight, he'd seen a dead body—a homeless man he was familiar with who had OD'd behind the Dumpster in the apartment where he was living. His grandmother had asked him to take out the trash and that's when he stumbled across the guy, huddled in a ball, a needle still sticking straight up out of his pale arm. He'd watched his oldest cousin Trey, Keenan's brother, slash a guy with a broken bottle because he thought he had stolen his phone. Although he was only cut in arm, Toby was sure that guy ended up in the hospital with stitches. And, man, there was so much blood.

But those were all things out of his control. They might freak Candace out, but more than likely, she'd understand. She'd probably feel sorry for him. It was the other stuff—the bad stuff *he'd* done—that would make her ask herself what the hell she was doing with him.

He'd lost count of how many times he'd shoplifted. For a while, when he was sixteen or seventeen, he was stealing things almost every day. Candy bars, cigarettes, and booze were usually the easiest to slip into his pocket and walk out with, but occasionally he'd snag something more expensive like a leather wallet from a department store or a pair of expensive shoes. And then, during one particularly angry summer as a preteen, he'd smashed the headlights and side mirrors out of thirteen cars parked along Hoover between Jefferson and Thirty-Second Street down by USC. He remembered how much rage he'd felt that night, how much jealousy toward all the rich kids whose parents buy their cars and pay for their education. It had felt cathartic to hear the glass shatter and watch the mirrors pop, then droop listlessly against the car doors. With every swing of the tire iron, he'd felt more and more giddy, more and more equal. If he couldn't have a car, or an education, or parents who wanted to help him, no one should. The following day, when he walked back down the cracked sidewalk along Hoover and saw the shards of glass in the parking spaces and the damaged cars that were still there, their owners blissfully unaware that they'd been targeted, he actually felt bad. And he'd never done anything quite that destructive again. After the car incident, he stuck to shoplifting, petty theft, and of course, boosting things like the motorcycle Keenan had been helping him with. The owner probably had insurance, so he'd be okay.

That brought Toby to a different thought: Keenan. Keenan was the only one who had stayed in his life. And that's why he was so loyal to him. All he and his cousin had were each other.

Candace? Well, there were certainly girls that

wouldn't bat an eye at Toby's tarnished past, and some would even get off on it. But Candace wasn't that type and he knew it. Candace was a good girl. She'd grown up in a world where parents hand their kids twenty bucks so they can go shopping with their friends. She'd dated boys that played sports and studied for midterms, not the type that trawl parking lots looking for unlocked cars. Bottom line, it was a crapshoot whether she'd come back and if she did, how long she'd stay. If she did, though, he vowed to do whatever it took not to scare her away.

"What do you mean you're *okay doing the other stuff*?" Keenan laughed dismissively. "Stolen bikes and catalytic converters? Come on. You only make, like, a grand a pop. It's not even worth the time."

Offended, Toby stood up. "I'll think about it, all right?" He knew if he continued to sit there that Keenan would keep grinding on him until he gave in.

"Think hard, cuz. Thirty grand is a lot of money," Keenan said under his breath. Without another word, Toby crushed his beer can and tossed it into the trash on his way back into the house.

Candace dropped her duffel bag on Toby's bed and darted into his bathroom. As she shut the door and turned on the shower full blast, she couldn't help but replay in her head the look on his face when he opened the door and saw her standing there. There was relief in his eyes. Then he slipped his thumbs through the belt loops of her jeans and pulled her hips to his.

"That took waaaaay too long," he'd said, and then kissed her.

Candace stripped off her clothes and felt to see if the water was warm yet. It wasn't, so she stood in the middle of the small bathroom staring down at Toby's toiletries on the counter. Spotting his cologne, she twisted the cap off the bottle and lifted it to her nose. As she inhaled deeply, she closed her eyes. *I love how he smells*, she thought. *It's woodsy and fresh and spicy all at once.* Putting the bottle back where she found it, she picked up his shaving cream and squeezed a dollop onto her finger. Then she rubbed it onto her skin. She wasn't sure why but she felt intrigued by everything he owned, as if examining every single item he used each day somehow brought her closer to him. Realizing the mirror had completely steamed over now, she set the shaving cream back and stepped into the shower.

As she let the water cascade down her back, she felt relaxed for the first time in a long time. There was no pressure here. No mother crying on the curb, no little brother sneaking into her room to play a joke on her, no father she could reach only by email. No one had any expectations of her here. Toby didn't judge. He liked her for who she was, and it didn't matter where she came from.

When she opened the door to the bathroom, she saw Toby perched on the edge of his bed, talking on the phone. "I can't go less than two Gs," she heard him say in a tense voice as he looked up at her. Candace could tell the sight of her wrapped in a towel, the long strands of her wet hair clinging to her shoulders, had made him lose his concentration.

"What?" he asked, turning away to finish the call. Candy grinned to herself, liking the power she had over him. She pulled her brush from her bag and started to untangle her hair as she kept an eye on him in the foggy mirror.

"Yeah, that's what I thought. Okay. See you then." Toby ended the call and tossed his phone onto the bed. Their eyes met through her reflection and he gave her a look of approval.

"I never said you could use one of my towels," he teased. "Drop it. Now."

She pretended to laugh. "Ha, ha, ha, ha." She

winked and unzipped her duffel bag. Searching for her little pink bottle of body spray, she tossed a few items aside. Black lace and bows caught Toby's attention.

"Hey! What's that?" he asked, and quickly snatched the bag away. He playfully turned it upside down and poured the contents of her bag onto his bed. Seeing the black lace bra and panties, he plucked them from the pile. Laughing, she tried to grab for them but he lifted them out of her reach.

"Hey, dick!" She made another futile attempt at grabbing them without losing her towel. Candace couldn't help but laugh as he teased her. She knew there was no way she could reach them if he continued to hold them high above his head, but she was having fun trying. Staring up at them, Toby examined the skimpy lingerie.

"Nice. Did you wear these for that douchebag ex of yours?" She could detect a slight tinge of jealousy in his voice.

"Wouldn't you like to know?" she responded without missing a beat.

"I'm more interested in if you're going to wear 'em for me," he said with a cocky grin as he gave them back to her.

"That depends," she joked. "My fee is a grand a night."

"I'd consider that a bargain." He lay back on his bed, folding his arms behind his head. "Go put 'em on."

Taking the bra and panties with her, she slowly walked back into the bathroom and shut the door.

EIGHT
DECISIONS AND DEAD ENDS

Candace lay next to Toby in bed, her finger tracing the outline of the tattoo on his chest. Her frilly little bra and panties were crumpled on the floor next to the bed. She liked how she felt with his arm around her; he had a way of making her feel safe. *I just slept with a guy I met less than twenty-four hours ago*, she thought. If people at school found out, they'd probably think she was slutty. *What a load of BS. No one's giving Ian a hard time for hopping from one girl to the next.* Besides, Candace thought, it didn't matter what anyone at school thought about her anymore. She was never going to see any of them again—except Avery, of course.

Those people, like her parents, were all part of her past. Up until her mom admitted she'd been adopted, her entire life had been a lie. No wonder she'd always felt so confused.

But not anymore. There was nothing confusing about Toby. He was the first person she met after discovering herself and there was some kismet in that, she thought. *I was meant to find out the truth about myself so that I could meet him as the real Candace.* Not the puppet Candace who was tied to her parents' lies. Then another thought came to her. *Oh my god, what if my name isn't really Candace?* What if she'd been named something else at birth and her parents changed it? What if she had come into this world as a Lindsay, or a Megan, or a Sierra? The more she thought about it, the more her parents' lies infuriated her. She hated them so much!

Candy felt her blood start to boil, but she decided to let her anger go and think about positive things— like her future. The future actually seemed pretty good at the moment. In addition to possibly having met the man of her dreams, she was finally going to be able to learn who she was. To do that, she'd have to find her biological parents—or at least one of them. She could do that. She'd seen more than a few TV shows where people were reunited with biological family members they'd never met. It usually worked out well. Sometimes on those shows the person even discovered that his parents had also been searching for him.

She wondered what her real mother and father were like and imagined the multitude of possibilities. It was actually fun to come up with theories. *I'll bet they're divorced. Or never married.* Maybe that's why her mother gave her up, because it was too hard to be a single mom. Maybe they were married, though. And her mother was some famous actress or model and because of her career, she traveled too much to be able to raise a kid. People had always praised Candace's acting ability. When she was twelve, she was the lead in the school play. Maybe she'd inherited her talent. Perhaps her father was famous too. Maybe they were a power couple of sorts. *We live in Los Angeles, after all,* she thought. *There are hundreds of celebrities who live here. It's not completely unrealistic. And how cool would that be? To suddenly be invited to Hollywood parties and red carpets and award shows? Pretty damn cool.*

But even as she was imagining the amazing A-list lifestyle she could lead, Candace couldn't help but think about how her mother had given birth to her brother, Andrew. Her father had been holding her mother's hand, breathing with her, telling her to push. She always imagined that the same was true for her. That her mom had been the first to hold her, been there to comfort her the first time she cried, but she wasn't. They let Candace believe that she was, but she wasn't. And that hurt.

Toby was lost in thought as he stroked Candace's hair. The plan that Keenan had pitched to him a few hours earlier was weighing on his mind. Pedro and Keenan were going to want an answer soon and he didn't have one to give them. He kept going back to the risk involved in pulling a stunt like that. Keenan made it sound easy, like a sure bet, but Toby knew there was no such thing. *The higher the score, the higher the risk.* It was a truth he lived by and he'd seen it play out time and again. That's why he preferred to stick with quick and easy scams, down and dirty crimes of opportunity. No premeditation. He just made sure he was always ready when a situation presented itself. Just like with Candace. He could've passed her sad ass up when he saw her standing outside the gas station last night. He could've simply lit her cigarette and went on his way.

But he didn't. He saw an opportunity and he seized it. He wasn't out looking for a girl to hang with and he certainly wasn't seeking a romantic relationship. *The best things in life come unexpectedly*, he thought. *They're not planned, they're not premeditated.*

Candace, Candace, Candace. She certainly made an impression. He had trouble getting her out of his head. He'd never felt that before but wasn't sure he wanted to fight it. One thing concerned him, though. He was pretty sure she was a helluva lot younger than the other girls he'd dated. He was hoping she was eighteen but knew there was a solid chance she wasn't.

Even so, how could this ever work out? The good news was that she hated her mother. He felt like an ass for being happy about that, but in truth, he was. He was convinced her mother would never go for Candace dating someone like him. From the way Candace described her mom and dad, he was sure they would want her to end up with some douchebag college boy. There was no point in trying to explain to them that he would do anything he could to make her happy. And she was happy with him, he thought. She seemed to be. He could tell by the way she rested her head up against his shoulder the past two nights. Candace wanted freedom.

She was a smart girl who didn't need her parents hovering over her every second of the day. Being away from them, with him, in a place where she felt loved and safe and free to explore who she really was, was better for her. And he wanted her to be the happiest person in the world. For the first time ever, the idea of someone relying on him didn't freak him out. He actually liked taking care of her.

The more Candace's mother doesn't want her to do something, he thought, the more she'll want to do it. And her dad, well, from what Candace said, it seemed like he was pretty much out of the picture, so he wasn't too stressed about that.

So what about Keenan's plan? What if they got arrested? Then there'd certainly be no future with Candace; he'd probably never even see her again. And rumor had it that Dawson had killed someone before—a guy that took an overly eager interest in Dawson's girlfriend. He up and left one day, completely disappeared and no one heard from him again. Toby figured the poor idiot was at the bottom of the Santa Monica Bay with a cinder block tied to his wrists. If this job was going to wind up getting them killed, it obviously wasn't worth it.

Then again, thirty thousand dollars would help him take care of Candace for a long, long time. He could take her to cool places. Maybe even on a vacation or—

"I wanna find my mom," Candace declared as she rolled onto her side and propped her head on her hand. "My *real* one."

Just the idea sent a surge of excitement through Candace.

"Why?" he asked. Candace was surprised.

"Why wouldn't I? I'm probably a lot like her." All the questions Candace had about herself might finally be answered.

"What makes you think that?"

"Huh? Because of genetics."

He shrugged. "I'm nothing like my mother," Toby stated. Candace studied him. She could see the resentment buried deep in his eyes, under layers of pain.

She paused and touched his hand. "Look, it all makes sense now. The reason I don't get along with my mom was because I'm nothing like her. I have a feeling that if I meet my real mother, everything is going to click in ways it hasn't before." Toby's mouth twisted up for a moment as if he didn't agree. "What?"

"Maybe you're right. Who am I to say?" Was he trying to shake her confidence? If so, it was working.

"You think it's a bad idea for me to try to find her?"

"Never said that. She could be great. Or she might not be. Or she might be dead. There's more than one possibility, is all.

"I'm just curious. It's not like meeting her is going to solve the mysteries of the universe or something." She could minimize her expectations to Toby, but Candace couldn't help but hold on to the idea that this woman was somehow the key she needed to fix all the things wrong in her life.

"So find her," Toby said.

"How would do I that?" Candace asked, truly unsure where to start. She didn't know her biological mother's name and neither did her parents. That is, if her mother was actually telling her the truth. Maybe she did know and just didn't want to share that information with Candace. She coiled her arm around Toby's bicep and snuggled closer, inhaling the faint scent of the cologne she'd sniffed in the bathroom. In the midst of all this uncertainty and turmoil, it made her feel at ease.

"Well, I guess you'd start with the adoption agency and see if they'd tell you." Toby gave a shrug as he suggested it and put his arm around her, so she could rest her head on his chest. "That's where I would start, at least."

A half hour later, as Toby paced around, working another deal on his phone, Candace sat at the kitchen table searching adoption agencies on his tablet. She had no idea which one her parents had used, and she wasn't about to call them to find out. For all she knew, she could have been born in another state, or even another country. *That's an interesting possibility*, she thought. *What if I was born in Canada or something? Or France? Or Italy?* For every question that popped into her head, Candace could feel her mind spinning with more. *What if my real mom doesn't even speak English? What if she speaks French or Italian or German? What if she lives so far away that I never get the chance to meet her?* Frustrated, she sat back and waited for Toby to finish his call.

"I know, I know," he said. "But fifteen isn't enough. If you wanna do business, it's at least eighteen."

As Candace listened to his response, she thought, *Man, Toby really knows how to negotiate to get what he wants. I need to learn how to do that. I need to look at every-thing as a negotiation, without emotion, and stay calm.* That was the hardest part—staying calm.

Then Candace had another idea. If she couldn't narrow down which adoption agency her mother had used, maybe there was some type of service or software that could. She decided to search "help me find my biological mother." A list of private investigators specializing in locating estranged family members came up. Some had photos of themselves and looked cheesy—like those old type of PIs with mustaches and big potbellies from noir movies where the investigators refer to themselves as "private dicks." She giggled a little, the thought of *private dicks* lightening an otherwise serious moment. Others had portrait-style photos of themselves with their families or pictures of them sitting behind desks, hard looks on their faces and framed photos of themselves in cop uniforms, much younger, turned toward the camera.

With renewed interest, she started clicking through the websites until she came to one PI who listed his fee. His name was Mike Foster, and he charged a thousand dollars to find a biological parent or child. From the photo of him on the home page, he looked honest enough—a little weathered and rough around the edges, but honest.

As Toby hung up, he seemed happy with the results of the conversation, so Candy turned the tablet around.

"Look," she said. "Private investigators who figure it out for you." Before she could say more, her cell phone rang. She looked down at the display and smiled. "Oh, it's Avery." When Candace had returned earlier with her phone charger and was finally able to plug her cell in, she saw she'd missed six calls from Avery, eight from her mother, and two from her father. *Ugh! Leave me alone!* "Hey," Candace greeted her best friend with a chipper note in her voice.

"Where have you been?" an angry Avery blurted out. "I've called you, like, fifty times!" Candace could tell she was at school; the sounds of kids laughing and talking filled the background.

"Just hanging out with a . . . friend," Candace said, and threw a little smile to Toby. He didn't notice. He was looking at the results she had found online.

"Who?" Avery demanded.

"You don't know him. He's a *new* friend." Candace saw Toby glance up at her and raise his eyebrow flirtatiously. She winked at him. She really wanted to refer to him as her new *boyfriend*, but that was a bit presumptuous.

"Well, your mom and dad are really worried about you. Your mom even came by the school to talk to me."

"She did?"

"Yes! And she talked to Ms. West and the principal and she even talked to Ian." She talked to Ian? *Good god*, Candace thought. *Now he probably thinks I ran away because I'm heartbroken that he's dating Miss Varsity Volleyball.*

"I can't believe she did that." Candace sighed, exasperated. "How do you know my dad's worried?" she asked, prompting Toby to look up again, mildly interested in the answer.

"He drove up here from San Diego. I just got off the phone with him. They reported you missing to the police. You need to call them and let 'em know you're okay!"

Candace was stunned, but she couldn't help but laugh. The police? "Oh my god . . . they're *psycho*!"

Avery didn't seem amused. "Everyone's worried, Candy."

Suddenly defiant again, Candace exhaled. "I'm not going home, so, I don't know, just call and tell 'em you talked to me and I'm fine."

"*You* need to call them." Avery was stern.

"Well I'm not going to," Candy retorted. "I guess they'll have to worry, then. Look, I gotta go. For all I know they've got the FBI tracing my phone."

"That's not funny," Avery replied. Candace could tell she wasn't impressed by the joke.

"Don't stress. I'll call you later."

"Candy! This is—" Candace tapped the button on her phone, ending the call before Avery could finish her sentence. She looked at Toby and shook her head.

"You just hung up on your best friend?" Toby asked.

"She does it to me, too. She'll get it over it." Candace felt a little guilty about hanging up on Avery but that conversation was going nowhere. She knew Avery wouldn't stop until Candace agreed to call her parents and there was no way she was doing that. Especially not after they'd decided to turn it into a major production.

"Apparently, my parents called the police," Candace explained as she took the tablet back, now more serious than she was with her friend. This fact concerned her. It was one thing for her parents to be calling around trying to find her, but now that the police were involved, she wondered if her plan to stay with Toby could be foiled more quickly than she anticipated. "I can't stand them."

Toby laughed. "The cops, huh? You little criminal. Maybe you *should* go home."

"Sick of me already?" she asked playfully. He

nodded. Giving him a little shove, she laughed too. "Screw you."

"Please do," Toby said, and wrapped his arms around her, pulling her closer to him.

"I told you. I'm not going back there. The next place I'm going is my birth mother's. If I can find her."

Before Toby could respond, they heard the door open and Keenan entered with a brown paper sack. As soon as he saw Candace, he smiled. "Hey there," Keenan said as he pulled a six-pack of beer from the bag. "Want one?" He gave each of them a bottle, twisting the top off Candace's before handing it to her like a gentleman.

"Thanks," she said, impressed.

"Candy, this is my cousin Keenan," Toby said, his voice a tad strained.

Keenan grinned, holding his gaze on her a little too long. "Nice to meet you. I came in to say hi last night but you'd already drifted off to la-la land."

She smiled, a little embarrassed. "Yeah well, that's Toby's fault. He was trying to get me drunk." She grinned at Toby to let him know she was teasing, but Toby's face was expressionless. Candace, unsure why Toby seemed so tense, went back to perusing the website.

"I'm about to go grab a burger. You guys wanna come?" Keenan posed the question to Toby but didn't take his eyes off Candace.

"We're good, dawg. Thanks anyway," Toby said abruptly. Keenan stood there a moment without saying anything, unspoken words passing between him and his cousin. Candace, uncomfortable, looked from one to the other. When she glanced at Toby, he looked down.

"Well," Keenan finally said. "See ya later, then."

As soon as he left, Candace asked quietly, "You didn't wanna hang out with him?"

"No. He can do his own thing."

Candace could sense that Toby was tenser than he was letting on. "How long have you two been roommates?" she asked, hoping he'd open up and tell her what was going on.

"Few months. Ever since he got paroled." Toby picked at the label on his beer bottle.

"Paroled?" The shock in Candace's voice was genuine. She had never met anyone who had been in jail before. It was sort of exciting in a weird way. "What was he in for?"

"The idiot knocked off a liquor store. Did three

years." Toby's tone was wrought with judgment. Candace reacted, surprised and a little intrigued. Never in a million years could she imagine sitting around with her friends, seriously planning the best way to rob a store. *Did he use a gun?* she wondered. *Was it just him or did he do it in a group? If it was a group, was Keenan the one in charge?* She pictured him with a stocking down over his head, leaning over the counter and demanding that the cashier fill a bag from the register. That's how it happened on those shows where they show surveillance footage from security cameras of mini-mart robberies.

"Wow. That's crazy." She didn't mean for it come off like she was impressed, but it did. When she saw the look Toby gave her, she instantly regretted saying anything at all.

"He's blood, so . . . I gotta help him out, right?" It was a rhetorical question. He said it as if he didn't have a choice. There was so much more Candace wanted to know about the situation between them but she didn't get a sense Toby would be forthcoming. She didn't want to press, but she couldn't help herself.

"He seems nice enough. Not someone I'd picture robbing a store," she said, hoping he'd elaborate on either Keenan or the crime.

"You don't know him," Toby said. "He's not a nice guy." Candace hated it when Toby would leave some vague statement just hanging in the air.

"Is that the only thing he's ever been arrested for?"

Toby almost laughed, "Uh . . . no. He's got a rap sheet that's been following him since he was thirteen. Mostly petty stuff, but a few that were more serious."

"Like what?" she asked, her curiosity soaring. "What's the worst thing he's ever done?"

"Done, or been arrested for?"

Candace paused, realizing that they weren't one and the same. "Done."

"Well . . . he and one of his brothers assaulted a couple of people one night when Keenan was . . ." Toby looked up at the ceiling, trying to remember his cousin's age. "I think he was about fifteen. Yeah, he must've been fifteen 'cause Gage was, like, twenty."

"What'd they do?" The hair on the back of Candace's neck went up as she rethought whether she even wanted to know. Assault was a pretty serious crime.

"I wasn't there so I don't know what really happened, but according to Keenan, he and Gage were standing in the alley behind some bar one night when this girl comes out all drunk. She's stumbling around on her heels and stuff and crying and yelling 'Fuck you!' and shit at the door. So Gage goes over and asks her what's wrong and she says she got in a fight with her boyfriend or whatever and I guess she was *super drunk*. Like she could hardly stand up and all that, so Gage starts kissing on her and feeling her up and the girl's telling him to get off her, leave her alone, and she tries to go back inside the bar but the door she came out of, it's an alley door, right? It's locked. So she's basically stuck there with Gage and Keenan."

"Okay . . ." Candace said apprehensively, knowing that the story was about to get worse.

"So Gage keeps going, even though this chick clearly isn't interested, and suddenly the door flies open and her boyfriend who she'd been fighting with comes out and sees 'em. He attacks Gage, they start going at it, and Keenan picks up a two-by-four from a trash pile and smashes this guy with it. It had a couple nails sticking out of it, so it cut his shoulder up."

"Wait," Candace said, stunned. "Keenan hit the boyfriend who was out there trying to help the girl?"

Toby nodded with disgust. "Pretty much. Somebody must've told the bouncer what was going on because he came out and that's when Gage and Keenan took off running."

Candace waited for more, but there wasn't any.

"The end," Toby said. "I think that's the worst thing he's ever done . . . at least the stuff I know about."

Candace exhaled, still processing the information she'd just learned. This was some serious shit. Assaulting a drunk girl? Beating up her boyfriend? Hitting someone with a two-by-four? When Toby said Keenan wasn't a good guy, he hadn't exaggerated.

"Why do you hang out with him, then? If he does stuff like that?" she asked, hoping Toby's apparent disgust at what Keenan had done wasn't an act he put on for her benefit. "I told you," he said. "He's blood. Besides that, we've always stuck up for each other. When no one had his back, I had it. When I needed something, he was the one who made sure I got it. I never said he was perfect," Toby responded, almost defensive. Candace watched as he crossed his arms in front of his chest and seemed to get lost in a memory. His blue-eyed gaze softened, as if he wasn't looking at anything in particular. She waited for him to speak again.

"I remember one time when I was living with him and my aunt and her boyfriend, Hank . . ." he began cautiously. "Keenan was eighteen and I was fifteen at the time . . . anyway, Keenan did something to piss Hank off and Hank beat the crap out of him. I mean,

Hank did that a lot, but this time was super bad. So at one point, Hank picks up this heavy ashtray that Aunt Patricia used to have on the coffee table. It was big, the kind they used to have in the fifties, I think." With his hands, Toby made a circle about seven inches wide to show how big the ashtray was.

"It was a really dense glass so it had some real weight to it. Hank grabs this thing up and just—wham!" Toby smacked his fist into the palm of his hand for emphasis. "He just clocked him right on the side of the head with it."

"Oh my god . . ." Candace said, not even thinking about the words before she said them.

"Keenan drops to the floor, out cold. Hank stands there like he can't believe he just did that. So I shake Keenan and try to wake him up but he's not coming to and there's blood coming out of his nose. The blood's what worried me the most. So I grab the phone to call 911 and Hank won't let me. He snatches it out of my hand."

"Why?" Candace asked. She couldn't fathom why someone would rather see a person die than let someone call an ambulance.

"Afraid he'd get in trouble, I guess. Anyway, I knew

that if he was hurt as bad as I thought, he didn't have much time, so I went after Hank. This guy was two hundred fifty pounds but I threw his ass up against the wall and told him that Keenan dies, I'd kill him. He knew I meant it, too, because he told me to take the phone. I called 911 and the paramedics came and got Keenan."

Candace could hardly believe the story she was hearing. She couldn't imagine what it must have been like for Toby to see his cousin lying there on the floor, the fear he must've felt believing he could die right then and there. Nothing like that had ever happened in her house. Her father had never hit her mother, or her, or Andrew. Fights consisted of slamming doors and the silent treatment, not smashing someone in the head with an ashtray.

Her heart went out to Toby. She was grateful he'd finally opened up to her a little, given her a tiny window into his past, helping her to understand who he was. She could tell that this was just one of many dark stories Toby had about his childhood. She could see it when she gazed into his eyes, but hadn't understood what it was she was sensing. Now she knew.

Candace rested her hand on Toby's. "I'm sorry," she said softly. "I guess you saved his life."

Toby instinctively pulled his hand away, retreating from their connection. "He's done the same for me," Toby said. "That's why he can live here as long as he wants." Then, Toby abruptly stood up and walked out of the room, leaving Candy there alone.

NINE
DARKNESS BRINGS THE UNFORESEEN

The vast Los Angeles cityscape stretched out for miles and then seemed to suddenly disappear into darkness. That was where the Pacific Ocean met the city's sandy coast, a chaotic mass of lights and freeways—and then nothing but deep, black ocean for as far as the eye could see. LA is an easy place to get lost, or to vanish if that's what you preferred, and many did. It was a mecca for dreamers—beautiful people arriving by the busload every day to become actors, models, screenwriters, and movie directors. They all come armed with a vision of their future and the willingness to risk it all. Most of them fail. They eventually give in to the flash and floss, or the drugs, or the fast lifestyle, while others give up and go back to wherever they came from to live the lives they tried so desperately to leave behind. Los Angeles is in fact, a city full of risk-takers who suck at calculating odds.

"This is really good," Toby said, and looked up. Candace had been anxiously awaiting his response. "I love that last part—'LA is a city full of risk-takers who suck at calculating odds.' That's completely true."

Candace grinned, soaking in the compliment. "Really?" she asked. "You like it? Or are you just saying that?"

"I have nothing to gain from kissing your ass," he said, and playfully grabbed the waist of her jeans, flipping her over on her stomach. "Although I will if you want me to." She laughed as he pretended to tug her pants down.

"I'm serious!" She laughed again. "I'm trying to understand why he gave me a seventy-three percent. I thought it was pretty good. Did you read what he wrote?"

Toby read the scrawled comment from her teacher on the front page in a deep, booming voice with a terrible British accent. "'This is an interesting foray into a character that needs to be better developed. Go deeper. Explain who she is and why she does what she does.'"

"Is that your literature teacher voice?" she asked.

"It's my stuffy, know-it-all teacher voice," he quipped back.

"You sounded so much like him, I thought he was in the room," Candace teased, and widened her eyes.

Toby chuckled, amused. "In all honesty, though, I think you're a great writer. Maybe this prick is just jealous."

"I doubt that. He's written two books that got published. What do you think he means by 'a character that needs to be better developed?'"

Toby pulled her on top of him and kissed her. "I think," he said while playing with a lock of her hair, "that some people have a hard time understanding what's right in front of them. People want you to do things a certain way, be a certain way, act like they want you to act. . . . There's nothing wrong with what you wrote. You're very talented."

Candace was touched by his words. So much so that she felt her heart expand in her chest. It didn't matter what her Lit teacher thought about her writing. Toby thought it was good; he got her writing and he got her. And he was right that everywhere you go, people are trying to mold you into what they want you to be. Her whole life had been that way. If it wasn't her parents, it was her teachers. They all wanted her to change what she did and how she did it. Toby never did that. He let her be herself and that's all she really wanted—to be free to explore life and who she was and to figure out what *she* wanted. Candace could be moody when she wanted, angry, impulsive, or sweet and loving and vulnerable. It didn't matter to Toby. No matter what she did, it didn't feel wrong. He never criticized her or tried to change her. And yet, he still called her bluffs. He saw through all the filters and it gave her permission to be herself. She couldn't get that feeling at home or at school or anywhere else. The only people who understood her were Avery and now Toby. And he got her even better than Avery did.

Candace made a vow to herself that she'd never try to change him, either. She'd just accept him for who he was. That was something she'd had trouble doing with Ian. Every time she was with him, there was something she'd wished he would change; from the way he kissed to the way he kept a comb in his pocket that she never once saw him use, she'd always wished for something different.

I was wrong to do that to him, Candace realized. *I criticized him too much, told him what to do. I won't do that with Toby. I'm promising myself right now to never try to change him.* Just the promise itself felt like a breakthrough for Candace. It was the first time she'd had any clarity about what she'd done wrong in her relationship with Ian. Then again, not trying to change Toby was easy—much easier than with Ian. There wasn't anything that bugged her about Toby. She thought hard, trying to come up with something that irritated her. Nope. Nothing came to mind. Toby was pretty much perfect. Perfect in every way.

"I thought we were going to play some poker and order a pizza." Keenan interrupted the moment by poking his head into Toby's room. He had a stack of playing cards in his hand that he flipped back and forth between his fingers.

"Have you ever played poker before?" Toby asked Candace. She shook her head.

"I'll teach you!" Keenan exclaimed with more excitement than a game of cards warranted, and disappeared as quickly as he'd come.

"Do you *want* to learn how to play?" Toby asked.

"Sure," she said. "Why not? Everybody learns to play poker at some point in their lives, don't they?" The idea of learning poker sounded fun.

Keenan was already kneeling at the coffee table shuffling the cards when Candace and Toby entered the living room.

"What kind of poker are we going to play here?" Toby asked as he and Candace settled into their places.

"I was thinking strip poker," Keenan said, and threw a wink to Candace as if they shared a secret Toby was unaware of. She couldn't help but giggle a little. She could see how Keenan could talk, or flirt, his way out of trouble when he wanted to.

"Five-card stud," Toby said. "And everyone keeps their clothes on."

Keenan exaggerated his disappointment and turned to Candace. "Why do you hang out with him? He's no fun."

Candace smiled and looked at Toby, who shook his head. Even after what Toby told her about the incident in the alley, it was hard to picture Keenan as someone who could be so violent and unpredictable. To her, it seemed like he never took anything too seriously.

"Just show her how to play," Toby said.

"I am, I am. . . ." Keenan said. "The object of the game is to put together the best possible combination of five cards. If you can do that, you win the pot." Candace listened to Keenan explain the game, chuckling every time Keenan threw a poisonous look at Toby for interrupting.

"When they're all the same suit, that's a flush." Keenan pulled five spades from the deck and laid them out on the table. "Now a straight is when the cards are in the right order. Seven, eight, nine, ten, jack would be a straight. They don't have to be all the same color."

"A flush beats a straight," Toby butted in. Keenan groaned and dropped his chin to his chest.

"Yo. Let her learn what the hands are first, okay?" Toby threw up his palms, surrendering. "Don't let him confuse you. Now, if the cards are in order and in the same suit, what do you think that's called?" Candace stared down at the ace, deuce, three, four, and five that Toby was laying out. All hearts. She had no idea. She was already having trouble remembering what was what.

"I don't know," she said. "A really good hand?" Keenan grinned, liking her joke.

"Come on, yes you do. Think hard. It's both a straight and a flush."

"A . . . straight . . . flush?" Candace guessed.

"Ding, ding, ding!" Keenan high-fived her. "See? I knew there were smarts in that pretty little noggin of yours."

"All right, come on. She'll figure it out as we play."

Toby scooped up the cards and began to shuffle them, expertly taking the attention away from Keenan.

After two hours of accidentally winning a few hands and losing most of them, Candace was happy when the pizza arrived. As Toby pulled a twenty from his wallet to pay the delivery guy, Keenan reached over and lowered Candace's cards so he could see her hand.

"No, no," he admonished. "See that, cutie? You shouldn't have gotten rid of your ten. You're set up for a straight."

"Game over," Toby said as he pushed the cards off the table and set the pizza down. He opened the box, releasing a cloud of steam. "Let's eat. I gotta meet that guy in a half hour." Toby pulled a slice from the pie, letting the cheese stretch as far as he could.

"What guy?" Candace asked as she grabbed her own slice, peeled a curling piece of pepperoni off the top, and popped it into her mouth.

"She can stay here with me while you go," Keenan offered nonchalantly with his mouth full.

Candace didn't want to stay with Keenan, but before she could object, Toby set his cousin straight.

"Nah, Candy's going to come with me," he said in a tone that suggested it wasn't up for discussion.

Candace shrugged to Keenan, secretly suspecting that Toby didn't trust his cousin to be alone with her. But whatever Toby's reason, she was excited to be going with him. Inviting her deeper into his world meant that he wanted her to become more a part of it, permanent. Keenan let out a good-natured sigh and collected the cards.

"That's cool, man," he said. "Pedro's on his way over anyway. He's gonna wanna talk to you at some point."

"I know," Toby responded as he grabbed Candace's hoodie hanging on a hook by the door and handed it to her. Slipping it on, Candace snatched up another piece of pizza for the road and followed him out to the garage where his pickup was parked.

"Where we going?" Candace asked with enthusiasm, up for an adventure.

"I'm selling my bike to a guy," Toby said, and climbed into the cab.

Candace peeked over the side of the bed and saw a motorcycle tethered securely inside. Hopping in on the passenger side, she stretched the seat belt across her chest. "Nice motorcycle," she commented. "Too bad you're selling it before I ever got a chance to take a ride on it."

"You've never been on the back of a bike before?" Toby asked, a little surprised.

"Nope." Candace let the word ooze from her mouth. "My mom always said it was too dangerous." Deep down, Candace knew her mother was right: motorcycles could be deadly, though she suspected that her mom also didn't want her hanging out with the type of guys who rode motorcycles.

"She's right about that, at least," Toby said as he pressed the button opening the garage. "You get into a car accident, chances are you're going to walk away from it. Get hit on a bike, chances are you *won't*."

If there was one thing she was learning about Toby, it was that everything he did was calculated, thoughtful. He weighed things. Nothing was spur of the moment.

"Is that why you're selling it?" she asked innocently. "Because it's too dangerous?"

Toby paused. He seemed to be somewhat thrown off by her question. "Yeah, I guess," he said as he turned up the radio loud enough to make it hard to converse. As they pulled out onto the street, Candace glanced around the dark neighborhood and heard the neighbor's dog barking. It was beginning to feel familiar now. She was content. *This is where I'm meant to be*, she thought.

A short time later, they pulled into a vacant lot some-where near Culver City. Toby messed with the radio as Candace sat quietly in the passenger seat.

"So, what are we doing here, exactly?" she asked.

Toby looked up, surprised. "What do you mean? I told you I'm selling my old bike to a guy."

"I know but . . . I mean, why *here*? In this creepy lot? Why doesn't he just come pick it up from your house?" she asked. If the ominous environment hadn't already made her feel guarded, then Toby's hesitation certainly did. She could tell by the way he avoided eye contact that he was thinking up an answer. Was he lying to her? What were they really doing out here?

Candace felt a hot, worried feeling in the pit of her stomach just like the one she'd had the night before. She hadn't thought much about the vulnerable situation she'd put herself in until she found herself alone with a guy she'd just met, in his room, in a neighborhood she'd never visited, with people who were all wasted or stoned. Since then, she'd felt nothing but comfortable with Toby—until now. Something just wasn't right about being out here in the middle of nowhere. There wasn't another soul around. On top of that, it was dark.

As the Metrolink train clattered along the overpass

above them, spilling light onto the garbage-lined street, Toby responded to her question as if it were the most obvious thing in the world.

"I don't let just anyone know where I live. You never know who might come back and rob you or somethin'."

Would anyone really want to rob his *house?* she wondered. She silently admonished herself for having such a snobby thought. So what if Toby's house was small and run-down? He had a nice TV and speakers and stuff. It wasn't like his possessions weren't valuable enough to steal. But if he was so worried about his things being ripped off, why wasn't he stressed about the parties he said he had almost every weekend? She'd gotten the sense that he didn't know the people roaming through his house that well. Why was he so paranoid about the guy buying the bike and so laissez-faire about all the shady party guests?

Instead of questioning him further, she decided that there must be some sort of logic behind it. Maybe he'd been robbed by someone he'd sold stuff to in the past. Either way, it was his deal and she wasn't going to tell him how to do it. She reminded herself that she was lucky just to be sitting next to him; lucky that he wanted to bring her a little deeper into his world.

"So," he said. "What's your plan? You still wanna find your real mommy?"

That was a whole different set of problems. Candace knew she couldn't go home, or at least, she didn't want to. If she truly wanted to understand who she was and where she came from, she needed to track down the woman who gave birth to her. She needed to see who that woman was, what she was all about, why she didn't want her.

"I don't really have another choice," Candace said, knowing that she did, indeed, have choices. She could forget this whole thing and go back to her life with Mom and part-time life with Dad anytime she wanted.

"What if she tells you to get lost?" he asked, emotionless.

"Then . . ." Candace said, thinking about her answer. "I will, I guess." She shrugged. It's not like she could force someone to get to know her if she didn't want to. But she preferred not to entertain that thought at all. For the time being, she was enjoying the scenario she'd made up. With everything in her life changing, she decided to stick to the version with the happy ending. Her mother would be as excited about their reunion as she was.

"I think the best way to find your mom is to hire one of those private investigators," Toby said.

"Except it costs, like, a grand. I don't even have enough money to put gas in my car right now." She wasn't exaggerating. With the exception of the seven dollars and change in her purse, Candace was completely broke.

"What if I helped you out?" he asked.

She turned to him, surprised. "Like give me a loan?"

"Yeah, I mean, I do it all the time, right? And don't worry. I won't charge you interest like I do those losers."

Candace smiled, feeling genuinely touched and shocked and guilty all at the same time. Was he really going to loan her that much money? Who does that? Especially for someone they just met? That's a lot of trust. The fact that Toby was willing to do that and had such a big heart made her feel guilty for the thoughts that had run through her head only moments earlier. *I clearly have trust issues*, she silently declared, vowing not to question him again.

"That's pretty awesome of you," she said, beaming. With the ability to hire a private investigator, she'd probably find her mom in no time.

"Don't get used to it," he said with a wink, teasing her. They were interrupted by the sound of a dark green coupe coming up the street. Toby watched the car as it turned into the parking lot. "That's him. Stay here," he said, and hopped out of the truck.

Candace kept an eye on the rearview mirror as two guys exited the car and helped Toby unload the motorcycle from the back. Then one of the guys handed him some cash, which Toby counted before nodding. The passenger pulled out a helmet, got on the bike, and sped off followed by the driver of the car. It all happened in less than five minutes and Toby was back in the pickup, money in hand, and in a fantastic mood.

"Done deal," he said with a smile. "Let's go party!"

Toby's pickup cruised down Sunset Boulevard on its way to West Hollywood. It was still early, only ten thirty, but the strip was already sizzling with frenetic energy.

"Where are we going?" Candace asked, her window open, the warm breeze whipping her hair away from her face. Toby was all smiles.

"I'm takin' you someplace good," he said.

"Where?" she countered, well aware that he wanted

to surprise her. What a roller coaster tonight had already been! She felt a connection to him that she'd never felt with anyone before. Not even with Ian. She'd told Ian that she loved him countless times, but had she? Candace was beginning to think that what she felt for Toby was love and what she'd felt for Ian was something much less. Was that even possible? To fall in love with someone after only a couple of days? It had to be. The excitement and thrill and passion and bond was so strong with them. With Ian, she'd had fun and then they'd each gone on their way. She never really missed him when they weren't together. She thought about him, and looked forward to seeing him, but she never quite felt this comfortable. With Toby, it was like she never wanted to be away from him. It didn't even matter what they did, as long as they did it together. "Where are we going? I'm dying to know!"

"You'll see," he said with a sparkle in his eye.

Caught up in his elation she leaned across the seat and began to kiss his neck. He smelled good, like sweat and cologne and cigarettes and leather. Candace moved slowly from his ear to his collar, lightly kissing every inch of his skin. When she reached a certain point right above his chest, he flinched slightly. She looked up curiously and Toby grinned.

"That tickles," he said. She laughed and sat back in her seat, where she could watch the bright lights that illuminated the Sunset Strip.

Ten minutes later, Toby's pickup stopped in front of one of LA's most exclusive clubs and he handed his keys off to the valet.

"They're never gonna let us in here," Candace warned, a little taken aback that he'd even consider trying. She glanced down at the tank top and combat boots she was wearing—hardly the outfit to wear to a club. "I'm sure they have a dress code."

"Won't know unless we try," he said confidently.

With an arm slung around Candace's shoulder, they marched up to the doorman who was perched on a stool in front of the huge glass doors. Candace caught a glimpse of their reflection, clearly showing off to the world that they were a couple, with the palm trees and traffic streaming behind them. Tonight, West Hollywood felt like the center of the universe.

"What's the cover to go upstairs?" Toby asked the doorman, who gave him a dismissive look.

"No jeans," he uttered in a gravelly voice.

"How 'bout her?" Toby asked. "She okay?"

"If she's got ID, she is."

Toby reached into his pocket and removed his

wallet. He counted out five twenties and folded them expertly between his fingers.

"Her ID is in the pocket of my other pants."

The doorman stared at him for a moment and then studied Candace. "You twenty-one?"

"Just turned last month," she said, trying to seem convincing. The doorman took the cash from Toby's hand and nodded inside.

"Top floor," he said as he slipped the money into his pocket. And off they went.

The lights of Sunset Strip glittered down below. Candace and Toby peered over the railing, taking it all in. "Look at the cars," she whispered. "All the red lights going away and the white lights coming toward us. It looks like they're all connected."

"It does look like that, kinda," he said. She watched as he slowly sipped and savored his drink in the same way he was savoring the moment. She was savoring it too. She tilted her head to the sky and inhaled the scent of nighttime. That's when she noticed the silence.

"It's weird how quiet it is up here," she mused. "You know that there's all kinds of noise down there . . . honking, yelling, music playing. But up here, nothing.

Almost like a movie with the volume turned off." He looked down at her and smiled. Inside the double doors, hipsters and rich foreigners and the Hollywood elite were dancing to a DJ, sprawled out on plush sofas, enjoying bottle service and trying to chat over the loud thumping of bass. But out here on the balcony, the night was calm.

"You deserve this, Candace," Toby said as he ducked under one of the hanging lanterns and relaxed in an oversize lounge chair. "You deserve somebody who can bring you to these kinds of places and treat you right."

She smiled. "Haven't I found him?" She lowered herself into the lounge chair next to him and cozied up under his arm.

Toby didn't answer. He just continued to stare off into the dark sky. Candace felt a tinge of doubt creep in. *Maybe he's telling me he's not the one*, she thought. As quickly as the thought came, she dismissed it. Toby was a complicated guy. Maybe he just wasn't ready to say what he was really feeling. As the moment grew awkward, she decided it was time to change the subject. "Which way is the ocean?"

He thought for a moment, then nodded west. "Santa Monica's that way."

They sat in silence. The heavy thoughts that plagued Candace's mind creeped back in. *We have so much in common, though*, she thought. They both wanted something more than they had, something that could help them define who they were. Los Angeles was a city of risk-takers, most of whom were destined to fail.

TEN
IN THE DARKEST HOUR

Sleeping Beauty, Toby thought as he gazed at Candace, snuggled up in his bed, wrapped in blankets. She was naked under the sheets and he could see the outline of her perfect form. An hour ago, they'd stared deep into each other's eyes as they made love and he felt even more bonded with her than before. He carefully reached over and touched her hair as it cascaded down the pillow. Sleeping Beauty? Or more like *Beauty and the Beast*? he wondered. He pushed away thoughts of the many ways he was bad for her. *I'm not going to be bad for her*, he told himself. *I can be everything she needs.*

The more he thought about it, the more his palms began to sweat, so he decided to go pull Candace's car into the garage. It had been on his mind since Candace told him her parents had called the police to report her missing. If they happened to drive past and see her car, they'd take her away. He didn't want that. He wanted her to stay.

Getting out of bed, he quietly opened Candace's purse on the nightstand and extracted her car keys.

Keenan was hanging out with a few friends when Toby walked through the living room and opened the door. "Hey," Keenan said as he stood up. "You going somewhere?"

"Just to pull her car into the garage."

"Why? Someone lookin' for her?" joked Randy, a short, stocky guy with full sleeves of tattoos. He knew Randy had no idea that his joke was actually the truth, so Toby chuckled, trying to play it off.

He started again for the door but Keenan grabbed his arm. "We need to talk," Keenan said, dead serious. Toby nodded, then continued outside.

Toby unlocked the driver's door to Candace's car, and as he pushed the seat back to make room, he noticed a little heart-shaped decoration hanging from the rearview mirror. He let the heart dangle into his hand. *Everything about her is so innocent*, he thought. *She doesn't belong here. She's going to get hurt if she stays.* Even if he could manage to protect her, this environment would eventually suck all the innocence and beauty out of her like a vampire. Toby glanced back toward the house. Even Keenan couldn't be trusted. Right now Toby worried whether he'd slipped down the hall and into his room. Was he lingering in the doorway, lascivious urges flashing through his mind as he watched Candace sleeping? With that unsettling thought at the forefront of his mind, Toby quickly pulled Candace's car into the garage and slid the door down, hiding it from the world. If he wanted Candace all to himself, he'd have to keep her safe. And that meant away from the police, away from Keenan, and away from the stolen bikes and petty crimes.

As Toby walked back into the living room, he was relieved to see that Keenan was still seated on the sofa talking to his friends. He flashed his cousin a quick look before heading down the hall to his own room. As he passed the bathroom, he could hear Randy say, "So where'd he find this bitch?" and knew Candace had been the topic of conversation.

Settling back down on the bed with Candace, he thought more about Keenan and Pedro's plan to make a fast thirty grand by ripping off Dawson. He didn't want to do it. Not just because it was risky, but because that was exactly the type of thing he needed to change about himself if he was going to have a future with Candace. He didn't want to be a low-life thug and criminal. He wanted to be the type of guy Candace could be proud of. But he also wanted to make enough money to make her happy. She'd been so happy at the club. He remembered looking over and seeing her sip a glass of champagne, holding the flute in her delicate little fingers. How could he ever afford to give her that life if he stopped selling hot laptops and televisions? A legitimate job was out of the question. He'd never finished high school and knew no one was going to hire him to do anything more than bag groceries or flip burgers. The peer-to-peer lending gig was okay, but it didn't bring in nearly as much as his criminal activity did. Plus, his resources were limited. There was only so much money he could loan out, and most of his time was spent waiting to be paid back.

Maybe one last big score wasn't such a bad idea. It'd give him enough cash to support himself and Candace for almost a year while he made plans to go legit. A year was enough time to find a job in construction or get his GED and take a few classes at a trade school.

To make matters more complicated, Toby knew if he said no, his cousin would blame his lack of participation on Candace. He could feel the tension with Keenan ever since he brought her home, and he wasn't sure if he resented her being there or just wanted her for himself. It didn't matter, though. He and Keenan were tight and they'd always promised never to let a girl come between them. That promise, of course, was made before Toby ever laid eyes on Candace.

Toby tugged at the blanket, pulling it up over Candace's shoulders. Then he glanced at the clock. Dawn was only an hour away. Deciding he'd better get some sleep, he closed his eyes and joined Candace in a peaceful slumber. He knew he'd have to give Keenan an answer soon, but that decision could wait. At least for now.

Get off the phone already, Candace silently pleaded as she and Toby sat in matching chairs across from the private investigator. Mike Foster seemed smaller behind his oversize desk than he should have at a significant 250 pounds. She looked around the room nervously as the detective continued his phone call. If someone had told Candace three days ago that she'd be sitting in the cluttered office of a private investigator trying to find her biological mother, she would have laughed. But there was nothing funny about this situation now. All she could feel was the swarm of butterflies in her stomach.

"Sorry about that," Mike apologized as he hung up the phone and ran his hands through his thick, graying hair. "I gave my secretary the day off cuz she was having morning sickness. I can't wait till she pops that baby out and can keep her breakfast down." Mike chuckled. Candace gave him an almost obligatory smile, wishing he'd just get to the heart of the matter.

"So," Mike said. "Do you know your natural mother's name?"

"No," Candace responded, worried it could be a problem. In the back of her mind, her biggest fear was that this aging detective would tell her that he couldn't help her, there was no way to find her mother, and she'd have to go through life wondering where she came from.

"How about the agency your adoptive parents went through?"

"I don't know that, either." Strike two. The anxiety was growing. Candace looked over at Toby, who gave her a little smile and a nod.

"That's fine," Mike responded. "It just makes my job easier, is all. How about your social security number? You know that?"

"Yes, right here." Finally! She could give him something to start with.

"Great." He seemed relieved as he passed her some paperwork and she dug through her wallet for her social security card. "Fill out as much of that as you can. Also . . . it'll be one thousand even."

Candace gave Toby a grateful look as he pulled out the cash to pay the man. She watched Toby count out the crisp hundred-dollar bills, all ten of them, into a pile on Mike's desk. It was so much money! She still couldn't believe Toby was loaning it to her. And he didn't hesitate. She loved the fact that he cared enough about her to help her this way. And she loved that she was able to do this with Toby's help instead of her parents'. *Toby's on my side.* It was a comforting thought.

Candace grabbed up one of the pens jutting from a coffee cup on Mike's desk and began carefully filling in the form. When she got to the address line, she looked at Toby quizzically. He leaned over to see what she was pointing to.

"Leave it blank," he said. Candace continued to fill

out the paper with her date of birth, her adoptive parents' names, and even Andrew's name and date of birth. She scribbled a little asterisk by his name and wrote *Not adopted, though*. Maybe that information wasn't important to Mike, but in any case, she wanted him to have it. It was important to her.

Candace signed the form and slid it to Mike as he printed a receipt for Toby.

"How long do you think it will take?" she asked, secretly wishing he'd have the information by tomorrow.

"Hard to say. Sometimes a day, sometimes a few months, sometimes a year. But usually within a few days. I've been doing this a long time and I'm pretty damn good at what I do." Mike's tone was just as cocky as his promise. But it made Candace feel better.

"Thank you," Candace said, and stood up. Mike shook both her hand and Toby's before walking them to the door. Despite all the worry and nerves, Candace had never felt more like an adult than she did stepping out of Mike's office. She'd signed her first real contract, hired a professional to do a job. That, in and of itself, was life changing. For the first time ever, she didn't need her mom or dad to do it for her. She'd handled it all on her own, and she was taking control of her life.

She felt strangely self-possessed and confident as they strolled through the parking lot to Toby's truck.

Candace pulled her door shut and looked at Toby.

"Well," Candace sighed. "That part's done. What now?"

"Now," Toby said, grinning, "we get lunch. I'm starving."

"Me too."

ELEVEN
ONE ITTY-BITTY MISTAKE

Candace stared out the window of Toby's pickup, watching the scenery speed by. "Do you really think he can find her within a few days? It seems like it might take longer than that."

"That's what he said." Toby shrugged. "But who knows? People lie."

Candace looked at him, appreciative. "It means a lot that you helped me out with the money. If it weren't for you, I'd probably never find my real mom."

"Don't thank me. It's just an advance on the money you're gonna pay back."

"Still," she said, and took off her seat belt, sliding across the seat. Snuggling close, she kissed him on the cheek. "You're pretty amazing," she whispered in his ear.

"All right, tough girl." He grinned. "That's enough."

The sudden ear-shattering shriek of a police siren prompted Toby and Candace to simultaneously look in the rearview mirror. It was coming from a cop car right behind him. Where'd he come from?

"Shit," Toby said. Candace quickly grabbed for her seat belt and slipped it back on.

Toby pulled to the curb remaining relatively calm, and turned off the car. Candace stared into the side mirror as the door to the patrol car swung open. She was terrified. Images flashed through her mind of being cuffed and dragged away from Toby, forced to go back home. *Please don't let that happen*, she begged the universe. *I belong with Toby.*

"What do we do?" she whispered, panic rising in her voice.

"Be cool," he said. "We don't know what he wants yet. Nobody can connect you to this truck, so it's not about you."

Candace's gaze flitted back to the mirror where

the tall African-American police officer, looking even thicker with his bulletproof vest, was exiting his patrol car. *Oh my god*, she thought as she saw him unsnap the strap on his holster.

Toby rolled down his window and looked up at the hulking figure who leaned down to take a peek inside the truck.

"License and registration, please," the officer said flatly. Candace just stared down at the floor, trying not to make eye contact.

Toby pulled both from his wallet and handed them over. The cop glanced from the license to Toby, to make sure the picture was legit. "Can I ask why you pulled me over, sir?" Toby asked, showing him the utmost respect.

Although Candace wasn't looking, she could see the officer lean to his right and knew he was staring at her. She finally glanced up at him and forced a smile.

"Passengers have to wear their seat belts at all times. That's a ticket." *Thank god!* Candace thought. *He has no idea who I am!* At the same time, she didn't want Toby to get in trouble. It wasn't *his* idea for her to take off her seat belt. Maybe she could mitigate this.

"It was my fault," Candace added quickly. "Please don't give him the ticket."

Toby turned his head and shot her a look telling her to pipe down. Although the officer couldn't see it, Candace could—there was anger in Toby's eyes. The cop leaned farther into the window and studied Candace a little too long. Finally, he took Toby's license and registration and walked back to his cruiser.

"I'm so sorry," she said as soon as the cop was out of earshot. She felt horrible. Now Toby was going to get a ticket that he didn't deserve.

"Keep your mouth shut, okay?" Toby said in a stern tone as he stared back at the steering wheel. Candace tried to touch his hand but Toby jerked it away and then looked directly at her. "You're gonna get us both in a lot of trouble." He shook his head in exasperation and turned his attention back to the policeman, who was now seated in his car, running the license. Candace slouched back into her seat, quiet. *He's mad*, she thought. *What if he's so pissed off he doesn't want to be with me anymore? What have I done? I'm such an idiot!*

The cop returned after what felt like an eternity. "Step out of the vehicle, sir," he instructed.

Toby, confused, obeyed orders. "What's going on?" he asked steadily as he stepped out of the car. The officer shut his door.

"Place your hands on the hood of the truck." Again,

Toby obeyed. Candace watched in horror as the cop frisked Toby. Toby made eye contact with her through the windshield as the officer knelt to pat down his legs. Although Candace was starting to panic, Toby appeared surprisingly calm. To Candace, it looked like the policeman was going to arrest him. But for what? He hadn't done anything wrong!

As the cop slid his hands up and down the front of Toby's jeans he asked, "Are you aware you're wanted on a bench warrant? Failure to appear on a DUI?" *What?* Candace was confused. *What's a bench warrant? What's he talking about? DUI?*

Toby instantly became defensive but maintained his composure. "My lawyer was supposed to take care of that."

"I guess you're going to need to sort that out with your attorney."

Candace continued to watch, confounded, from inside the truck as the cop placed Toby in cuffs and led him to the back of the squad car. He didn't do anything to resist. She had no idea where they were taking him or what to do. Then the officer returned to the vehicle on the passenger side.

"Open the door and step out of the car, miss." Fear

gripped her throat as Candace slowly opened the door and got out. "Do you have ID on you?" he asked. She nodded. "Get it, please."

She reached back into the truck and pulled her driver's license from her purse. "Have a seat there on the curb," he said as he took the license. "I'll be back in a minute."

Candace could tell she was shaking as she sat there waiting. The glare from the sun made it impossible to see Toby in the backseat of the squad car. *He's going to find out I've been reported missing now. It's over. All over.* She didn't care about the trouble she'd be in with the police or with her parents. All she could think about was whether this was the last time she'd ever get to see Toby. What if he went to jail? She couldn't even picture him behind bars in one of those baggy orange jumpsuits. Toby wasn't a criminal! He didn't belong locked up with thieves and drug dealers and murderers. She clasped her hands together to keep them from shaking, but as soon as she did, she could feel tears forming in her eyes. *This can't be the end*, she thought. *It's just the beginning.* The beginning of her new life with Toby and her real mother and discovering who she was meant to be. How unfair that she could get everything she wanted and have it all stripped away two days later. *Damn them!* Candace cursed her mom and dad. *This is their fault for reporting me missing! I hate them so much!*

Candace held her breath as the officer returned and handed her back her license.

"Miss White, are you aware that you've been reported as a runaway?"

TWELVE
LITTLE GIRL FOUND

Candace used her sleeve to wipe away the occasional
tear that ran down her cheek. She leaned back against
the wall of the holding cell, looking at a boy about
Andrew's age who sat on a bench opposite her. They'd
taken her shoes and her purse and her hoodie before
locking the cell door closed. She was sure they were
calling her parents, telling them that their missing
daughter had been found.

She wondered what it must be like for Toby right
now. Was he in a cell here too? Or had they taken him
away someplace else?

"Candace White?" a lady officer said as she unlocked the cell door. "Your parents are here."

Candace's heart sank as she stood up and followed the woman through a corridor and was buzzed through a door to the lobby. The room was full of people and Candace didn't immediately see her mom and dad until she heard her mother yell, "Candy!"

Candace recoiled as Shannon rushed over and threw her arms around her. Candace had no interest in returning the hug. It felt like her life was over. She was numb.

"We were so worried about you!" her mom said, the relief coming through in her voice. "I'm so glad you're safe!"

Candace followed her mother to a bench where her father soon joined them, carrying a plastic bin with her shoes, hoodie, and purse. She could tell from the way he dropped the bin down in front of her that he was angry. Without a word, Candace started to put on her shoes, dreading the interrogation she knew was coming as soon as they got into the car.

"I'm here to post bail for my cousin." Candace heard the familiar voice and looked up to see Keenan standing at the counter. Her heart skipped a beat as she quickly looked back down, careful not to let on that she knew who he was. *Toby's here*, she silently rejoiced. At least she knew where he was and that he was going to be bailed out. Thank god they hadn't carted him away to county jail or something.

Candace nonchalantly gazed up again and saw Keenan looking at her. They exchanged a brief glance and both turned back to what they were doing, keeping their secret. It worked. Her parents had no idea there was any connection between them.

"Let's get out of here," Kurt said as Candace slid her arms into her hoodie and grabbed her purse. Candace was silent in the car on the way home, refusing to talk at all about where she'd been or who she'd been staying with. She knew they'd be furious if they learned anything at all about Toby, and she wanted to make sure she didn't get him into more trouble than she already had. Needless to say, this just infuriated her parents, and by the time they arrived home, she could tell they'd both had it.

"We *are* going to talk about this whether you want to or not, Candy," Kurt said authoritatively as they walked from the car to the front door. Candace just let out an exaggerated sigh.

Andrew, who had heard the door open, came rushing down the stairs and threw his arms around his older sister, almost knocking her over. Candace couldn't help but smile a little. She hadn't realized it but she'd actually missed the little pest, and it was nice to be welcomed home instead of bitched at.

"Candy! You're back! I missed you so much!" Andrew said as he tightened his squeeze on her. *Damn, he's getting strong*, she thought.

"Andrew, honey, your dad and I need to talk to Candy alone, okay?"

Andrew continued to hold Candace. "Don't leave again, all right?" As he looked up at her, she could see the glimmer of fear that lingered in his eyes and she knew he'd been worried about her too.

His plea touched her, but she wasn't going to make any promises. All she could think about was whether or not Toby would ever talk to her again. She felt incredibly guilty for putting him in the situation he was in. If she hadn't taken off her seat belt and leaned across to kiss him, they'd probably be back at his place right now, chilling. She wasn't sure what the whole thing was with the bench warrant and the DUI, but from Toby's reaction, she gathered there was some type of mistake involved. From what she'd seen, Toby had been nothing but responsible. Even after he took her to the club on Sunset, he stopped drinking about an hour before they left so he'd be okay to drive. When she'd asked him why he didn't want more champagne, he'd told her that it was up to him to make sure they got back in one piece.

"You think I'd do something to jeopardize that pretty little face of yours?" he'd asked as he caressed her cheek. "I'm going to take care of you. . . . You know that, right? You'll always feel safe with me."

Candace did feel safe with him. She trusted him implicitly. Even though it was a short time to know and trust someone, the chemistry they had was stronger than she'd ever felt with anyone before. At least it had been. All she could think about now was whether he'd be so upset that he'd want nothing more to do with her. She couldn't bear the thought of that and the only thing she wanted to do was call him and see if he'd answer his phone. But she couldn't do that because she had her parents breathing down her neck, demanding details that she knew she couldn't give.

"We'll chat later, okay?" Candace whispered to her little brother, who still gripped her in a bear hug. Andrew let her go and reluctantly went into the other room.

Her father repeated the question he'd already asked

twice on the car ride home. "Enough with the silent treatment, Candy. Time for some answers. Who was the guy you were arrested with?"

"Have you been staying with him?" her mom chimed in. *Well this is interesting*, Candace thought. She hadn't been yelled at by both parents at the same time since before they split. It felt the way it used to.

"No," Candy lied. "He was just a nice guy who gave me a ride. I'd never met him before." On the way home, she'd concocted a complex story about where she'd been staying and what she'd been doing, and none of it involved Toby. She was going to say she'd slept in her car and snuck in to the local YMCA to take a shower.

"You got into a car with some guy you don't even know?" Her mother gasped, wringing her thin hands together.

Candace crossed her arms and gazed off into the distance, pointedly tuning them out. *This is exactly why I bailed out of here*, she thought. *My parents will never understand. And yes, I did get into a car with someone I didn't know and guess what? He's amazing and he's helping me find my mom and I'm totally head over heels for him.* She knew she couldn't say any of what she was thinking, though, so she chose to plead the Fifth and say nothing at all.

"Where's your car, *Candace*?" Kurt asked. He only called her Candace instead of Candy when he was really pissed off. *Crap!* she thought. She'd forgotten about the car. It was still parked in Toby's garage, and she knew she couldn't be honest about *that*.

"I loaned it to someone. I'll get it back," she said, weaving the car into the lie she'd already committed to.

"Who did you loan it to?" her dad asked.

"You don't know him!"

"I want a name. *Now*," her father said in a deep voice. It was obvious he was coming to the end of his patience.

"Where have you been for the last two days?" her mother demanded.

There was no way Candace was going to answer that question. As a matter of fact, she wasn't going to answer any more questions at all. Turning on her heel, she completely ignored her mother and started to head for the stairs.

Irate, her mom grabbed her arm and spun her back around. Candace's eyes widened with shock and she yanked her arm away. She couldn't believe her mother actually grabbed her! She'd never done that before.

"Keep your hands off me!" Candace screamed, and raced up the stairs.

"Candy!" her father called out. Candace stopped midway up and turned to look at him.

"What? I hate her!" she yelled. As the words came out, all the pain and anger she felt toward her parents, all the guilt she felt about Toby, all the anxiety that he'd never want to see her again, came boiling to the surface and she couldn't hold back the tears. Sobbing, she went into her bedroom and slammed the door.

As she leaned against the door, she could hear her mother say, "She can't just do whatever she wants!" *Yes, I can!* Candace thought. *And there's nothing you can do to stop it!*

Candace pulled Mike Foster's business card from her purse and entered his numbers into the phone. It had been less than five hours since she'd hired him but she was desperate to find out if he'd made progress. Once she found her real mother, she could leave her parents behind for good.

Mike's line had just started to ring when she heard a loud knock on her bedroom door. Candace quickly hung up, not wanting her parents to know who she was trying to call. She slid the business card between her mattress and box spring.

"Candy, can I come in, please?" her father asked. Candace just wiped her eyes and sat in silence. She didn't want to talk right now to anyone except Mike Foster or Toby.

Kurt entered and stood in the doorway. Candace was waiting for him to yell at her, but instead he sat down next to her on the bed. "Talk to me, sweetie," he said.

"There's nothing to talk about," she said in a monotone voice. "You guys lied to me. I'm not your kid. That's all there is to it."

"Your mother and I both love you. We always have."

"Mom doesn't love me," Candace said without thinking. "Things were better when you were here." Deep down, she wanted her father to regret breaking up the family, to realize that he was partly responsible for how tense her relationship with her mother had become since he left.

"You're not being fair to her. She's been worried sick that something happened to you. She was in tears when she called me."

"I can't do this with her anymore. She wants to control everything. You know how she is. Of all people, you should understand why I want to get away from her. She used to nag at you the same way." Candace thought her father would agree but he gave her an ambiguous look.

"Your mother did complain a lot when we were together, but I gave her a lot to complain about. There was a lot going on between us that you and Andrew don't know about. And you don't need to know. She didn't drive me away. Our marriage had been falling apart for a long time, and she was actually the one who tried to hold it together after I gave up." Candace felt her heart sink in her chest. It made her angry that her father would take her mom's side. All this time, she'd held on to the fact that her mother had annoyed her father the same way she'd annoyed her. Everything was her mother's fault. "Your relationship with your mother is different from mine. She's been a great mother to you. The best. And what you're doing to her is completely unacceptable." His words made Candace feel even angrier and guiltier than before. Now her father was basically calling her a failure too? Telling her that she was the one being unfair? Screw him. He could've told her she was adopted but he didn't. He was just as culpable in that sense as her mom was.

"I'm always the one who's wrong, aren't I?" she hissed with contempt.

"No. You're right that we should've told you about the adoption earlier. We made a mistake and we both wish we would've handled it differently. But screaming at your mom and brother and disappearing for two days is not the way to handle it. You need to let go of this anger you have toward her. She doesn't deserve it."

"How would you know what it's like? You're not even here." She hoped her words would hurt him. She wanted him to feel as bad as she did. No one ever seemed to feel as bad as she did.

"Do you want to live with me? In San Diego?" The question surprised Candace. Now? *Now* he's inviting her to live with him? He'd never offered that before. Last week, she would have jumped at the chance. But now, everything was different. She'd met Toby. And she was on a mission to find her real mom. Candace didn't belong in San Diego with her father anymore. She belonged by Toby's side.

"I don't know what I want," she lied.

Her dad nodded. "Put some thought into it. But know this . . . I love you more than anything. So does your mom and Andrew. It doesn't matter who gave birth to you. You're *our* child, part of *our* family. See, when we first got married, your mother wanted a baby so badly. She—"

"I don't want to hear this. I really don't," Candace interrupted, trying not to tear up. She'd made her decision to separate from this family and find a new one. She knew hearing stories about how much they loved her and about how happy they were when they picked her up from the adoption agency or whatever would just make her feel conflicted. It was better to move on and never look back.

Her father was a little taken aback. "Well, when you're ready to hear it, I'll tell you," he said in an almost soothing tone. She nodded without saying anything else. He kissed her on the forehead and stood up.

"Are you leaving now?" she asked. A part of her wondered if her running away had maybe somehow made her parents realize they wanted to get back together. Maybe the scare of losing a child had jolted them enough that they'd united under a common cause. It wouldn't change anything for her, but at least her little brother would have his parents together again.

"Tomorrow morning. I want to spend a little time with Andrew, grab a pizza or something. Do you want to come?" Candace was disappointed. Even running away wasn't enough to make her father want to come back to the family. If what he'd said was true, that her mother had been the one trying to keep their marriage together, then why didn't he try harder? It was too much to take in. And what good would it do anyway?

"Not really." The idea of pretending to be one big happy family when they were anything but seemed fake and trite, and Candace wanted nothing to do with it.

"I would really like the four of us to go out and have a nice evening. Will you please do that?" *Why bother? Does he somehow think sharing a greasy pepperoni pie would fix everything that's broken in our family? He can't be that stupid.* But she knew the only way she'd ever get back to Toby was if she played by the rules and made it seem like she wouldn't run off again first chance she had. She needed them to leave her alone long enough that she could plan her escape. And this time, it would be permanent. Agreeing to this ridiculous pizza outing might help. Anything to get her back to Toby as quickly as possible.

"Fine," she replied. "I'll go, but I'm not going to pretend to have a good time."

"Fair enough," he said.

Candace was relieved when her dad walked out,

leaving her alone. She fell back onto her bed, closed her eyes, and inhaled deeply. A *cleansing breath*, they had called this in that yoga class. That's what she needed right now. To cleanse away the tension and anger and find a peaceful place where she could imagine life with Toby.

She pictured them together at the water park. They were splashing each other in the wave pool, laughing as the hot sun beat down on their faces. The muscles in Toby's chest and arms rippled as he reached out for her wrists and pulled her effortlessly toward him. His skin was warm under her touch. He wrapped his arms around her and kissed her as strands of her wet hair clung to the stubble on his face. There they were, amid the chaos of children playing, the waves lapping against their hips, without a care in the world. As Candace wrapped her legs around Toby's waist, she felt nothing but happiness. *We* are *going to have this moment*, she promised herself. For the first time ever, she knew what she wanted. She could picture it clearly. Her heart ached for it.

Candace picked up her phone and stared at the dark screen. She wanted to text Toby but had no idea what to say. She wasn't even sure Keenan was able to get him out of jail, and she certainly didn't want some nosy cop reading her text. Was he mad at her for getting him arrested? *It's better to wait*, she thought. *Be patient and let him make the first move.* She wanted to reach out to him so badly—to know that everything was okay between them. She set her phone down and drew her knees into her chest. Waiting was torture.

"That idiot DUI lawyer! He said he took care of it," Toby muttered, and looked out at the mass of traffic on the 110 freeway.

"I always say you can't trust those guys. They act like they're your friend but they're not," Keenan commiserated. For his cousin's sake, Toby made it seem like he was pissed off about the court fees and inconvenience, but deep down, he was more frightened than he was angry. Candace had been whisked away into the juvenile holding area as the officer took Toby to booking. The whole time Toby had been getting his fingers printed and his mugshot taken, his mind had been on her. He knew she was scared. He'd seen the terrified look in her eyes as they escorted her through the door when she threw a glance back at him, begging for him to do something. But there was nothing he could do.

She would be fine in juvenile custody. It was highly supervised and most of the kids in there had been caught tagging or skipping school or shoplifting. They weren't hardened criminals like the kind at county jail or the state prison. But even so, he'd wanted nothing more in that moment than to hold her in his arms and whisper that she'd be okay.

That wasn't the part that scared Toby, though. The thought that he might never see her again was the one thing he couldn't shake from his mind. It made him sick to his stomach. How had his life changed so much in three days? He wasn't sure, but it had. Ever since he brought her home from the gas station with that flimsy chocolate rose in her hand, everything had been different. For the first time he could remember, he felt hopeful. Daydreams that maybe *he* could have all the things that other people seemed to have drifted in and out of his head, making him feel at peace. Now he felt nothing but anxiety as he imagined what Candace's parents were saying to her.

If she'd told her parents anything about him at all, he knew they'd never let her get anywhere near him again. He wasn't a bad guy. He hadn't committed armed robbery or assaulted anyone. Yes, he'd been arrested for driving drunk several months back, but he'd been super responsible about taking care of that. And sure, he'd done a lot of bad things in his life, but he was trying to change. That first night when Candace was drunk, he'd made sure nothing happened between them. He'd loaned her money and gone with her to vet the private investigator she'd found. Those were all things that good boyfriends do. She'd inspired him to be better than he'd ever been before, and he knew that he had it in him to be a good guy.

It didn't take a genius to know that her parents wouldn't see it that way. They'd see him as an older guy with a record who was trying to corrupt their under-age daughter. He was sure they'd do whatever it took to ensure Candace was never in the same room with him again. *Just like Cara's parents*, he assumed. Cara was his first love, a girl who went to his school when he was twelve years old.

"I'm going to say this only one time," Cara's father had said as he unbuttoned his suit jacket. "Pretend you never met my daughter. Push every thought you have of her out of your head. There are lots of girls out there. Pick a different one."

Toby remembered how her dad's eyes bore into him

as he said it and how he gave him a forceful pat on the back before he walked away, leaving Toby feeling helpless. The pain of losing Cara had been almost as bad as the humiliation of being forced to give her up because her parents thought he wasn't good enough. He could still feel that resentment deep inside of him, hidden in a dark place in his heart that he never revisited.

I can't let that happen with Candace, he thought. *Not again.* Not with someone he cared for a hundred times more. *If I have to fight like hell to get her back, I will.*

Toby was still thinking about how he could find Candace and bring her back when Keenan pulled into the driveway.

"Thanks for bailing me out, man," Toby said, preoccupied as they walked toward the front door. "I'll figure out a way to pay you back real soon."

"Nothin' thirty K can't fix, right?" Keenan turned back and gave Toby a serious look as he slid his key into the lock. Toby hesitated as Keenan opened the door and let him enter first. Without a word, Toby walked down the hall to his bedroom.

As he kicked off his shoes and poured himself a shot, he continued to ponder his cousin's statement. All this time he'd been thinking that he should say no, that it was too risky, that if something went south, he could lose Candace forever. But maybe he'd been perceiving it all wrong. Given what had happened, maybe robbing Dawson with Pedro and Keenan was the exact thing that could bring Candace back. That thirty thousand dollars was more important than ever. Not just to repay his cousin the bail money, but now if he wanted to be with Candace, they'd probably have to run off together. Go someplace *far* away where her parents and the cops wouldn't find them. *Starting over takes money*, he thought. *Thirty thousand is enough to make that happen.*

Toby picked up Candace's shirt from the floor where she'd left it. He inhaled her scent and pictured her seated on the floor that first night, eyes closed, singing to Bob Marley. He'd liked observing her as she got lost in the moment. He remembered that he'd done the same with Cara.

Seated in the back of the classroom, he'd never spent any time listening to the teacher. Instead, he watched Cara, silently observing how she used the tip of her pencil to push her jet-black hair away from her green eyes. And how her nose scrunched up slightly when she was trying to think of an answer to the teacher's question.

He knew every one of her mannerisms so well that he could predict them.

Toby delicately folded Candace's shirt and mused at how much he'd learned about women since he first dated Cara. At twelve, he had no idea what it meant to be a boyfriend, but he'd tried to be a good one. He bought, and sometimes shoplifted, gifts for her. He didn't have money to get her flowers so he took a pair of scissors to school with him one day and on the walk home, he jumped the fence into the yard of the only house that had a thriving tulip bed and cut his own bouquet. When he gave them to her, she'd had the same sparkle in her eye that Candace had when he'd offered to pay for the private investigator. He loved seeing that look of surprise and joy, and knowing he'd done something right.

He remembered when Cara's parents found out that they were "going out" and forbade her to see him. She'd told him that her mom and dad knew of his cousins, including Keenan, and the reputation they all had of getting into trouble.

"But I'm not like them," Toby had said, panicked. "I don't get into trouble like that. And I'm going back to live with my grandma again, and she's really nice and she goes to church and everything." His desperate plea was more than just an attempt to get her back. It was the truth. Toby had just found out he was being sent to his grandmother's house, once again bounced around. At least this time he didn't mind.

"I'm sorry," Cara had said with a tear in her eye. "I like you. But they're my parents. I can't talk to you anymore." Cara walked off before he could say anything else. When he went to her house after school that evening, riding his bike almost twelve miles to get there, that's when her father met him at the door and told him to "pick someone else."

Toby rolled over and saw Candace's backpack leaning against the wall. He dumped it out and gently looked through her things, opening the makeup cases and smelling her body spray. It made him feel close to her. He imagined her coming back and flopping down on the bed and giggling as he tickled her.

That's what I want, he thought. *I'll do whatever it takes to get her back. And if I have to help Keenan and Pedro rob a drug dealer to get it, the risk is worth it.*

The obnoxious sounds of video games and Top 40 pop tunes were giving Candace a headache. *This is what hell must be like*, she thought. *A pizza joint with your family*. Andrew was over at the pool table trying to find out when the people playing would be finished so they could use the table. She'd already suffered through a game of air hockey and skee ball. Would it never end? She'd been trying all evening to break away for a few minutes to call Toby, but her captors were keeping a close eye on her. She'd even tried to go to the restroom alone only to have her mom jump up and declare she needed to use the little girls' room too.

She looked around the room at all the happy parents with their über-excited kids, and felt like an outsider. *I'll bet a thousand dollars that none of these kids are adopted.*

Before her parents' divorce, her family went out for pizza once a month. Everyone was given twenty dollars to play video games or the jukebox or whatever they wanted, and they'd spend hours there, just shooting at aliens or driving virtual race cars, and stuffing their faces full of Brooklyn-style pie. It was something she could always count on happening. She'd taken that for granted. She'd never thought for a moment that someday her parents would split, and these simple, monthly outings would be over.

Just like that, in the blink of an eye, they were no more. And nothing would ever be the same again.

"They're done!" Andrew announced. "Come on, let's play!"

Her mom and dad put down their pizza slices and got up. "Aren't you coming, honey?" her mother asked Candace.

"I hate pool."

"Please?" Andrew pleaded. "I want you on my team." As irritated as she was at her parents, it was hard to say no to Andrew's goofy little face.

"All right," she said, folding. "One game."

Andrew let out a whoop and dragged her over to the pool table, their parents trailing behind them.

After racking the balls Andrew sank one in the corner pocket and did an embarrassing little victory dance. As he walked around the table sizing up his next shot, Candace's cell phone rang. It was Toby. Excited, she set her cue down and headed toward the restrooms.

"I have to take this," she shouted back over her shoulder.

"Who is that?" her mom asked, worried.

"Avery."

Instead of going to the bathroom, Candace slipped out the restaurant's back door and planted her bottom down on a plastic chair the employees presumably used during their breaks.

"Hey, I'm glad you called," she said, answering the cell. "I thought maybe you were pissed at me."

She could tell Toby was using the Bluetooth in his truck. She could hear the din of traffic in the background. He seemed to be in a better mood now. His tone was light. "For getting me arrested? Why would I be mad about that?" He chuckled. Thank god! He wasn't mad at her. *Thank you, thank you, thank you!*

"I'm sooooo sorry," she said, genuinely meaning it.

"I'm just giving you a hard time. It has nothing to do with you. My lawyer messed up big-time. I would've called you earlier but I needed to clear my head a little. You know?"

"Yeah, I totally understand. I've been doing the same."

"I was worried about you. No one hurt you in jail, did they?"

"No."

"Good. As I was sitting there in that cell, all I could think about was if you were okay. I asked about you. They wouldn't tell me anything. I felt really helpless." Candace's heart swelled. "Then Keenan said he saw you leave with your parents so I knew you were safe. Where are you right now?"

"I'm at a restaurant with my parents and my brother pretending to be a big happy family. It's disgusting," she said, wishing she was with him instead.

"Playing 'good little girl,' huh? You miss me?"

Candace twirled a lock of hair around her finger. "Maybe. . . ."

"Well maybe I miss you, too. Except for that drooling thing you do when you're asleep. I don't miss *that*."

"Ha-ha," Candace said, deadpan, even though she was amused. "I just need to play it cool until I can get out of here again." Now that she knew Toby wanted to see her, the plan of regaining her parents' trust and earning enough freedom to skip out again was even more important than before.

"When will that be?"

"I'm on total lockdown, so probably not till tomorrow at least." With her father in the house, she knew it would be impossible to get away.

"It's all good. Call me if you want me to pick you up. Your car's still at my place."

"I'll figure it out."

"All right, gorgeous. G'night."

"'Night."

Candace ended the call feeling both relieved and

anxious. She was thrilled that Toby didn't blame her for the day's fiasco with the police and couldn't wait to see him again. She knew it wouldn't be easy to escape from Kurt and Shannon's Central Jail, but she was already forming an idea. . . .

THIRTEEN
THE CALM BEFORE THE STORM

The next morning, Candace was up early. In that foggy moment between sleep and consciousness, she'd remembered the three hundred dollars she'd earned by walking dogs the previous summer. Her mother had refused to let her get a summer job. She wanted her to focus on the chemistry class she was taking in summer school after getting a C in it the semester before. But Candace wanted to do something fun and earn some money that she could spend any way she wanted, so she'd answered an ad without her mom knowing. For seven weeks, she'd snuck out around lunchtime to take two poodles and a shih tzu around the block. Sure that Shannon would want to know where the money came from, Candace had hidden it in the pocket of a pair of old jeans on the top shelf of her closet. She'd pulled it off, too. Not only had she managed to keep the secret from her mom, she'd scored an A in Chem the second time around.

Pulling the pants down, she dug into the pocket and smiled. The rolled-up bills were still there. She also folded a few pairs of panties and a couple of tank tops and slid them into the pockets of her hoodie. She knew she couldn't put any clothing in her bag just in case one of her parents decided to rifle through it before she left for school. Her backpack was still at Toby's, but if anyone asked, she was ready to tell them it was in the trunk of her car. She was surprised they didn't press when she told them she'd loaned it to a friend. She guessed they figured it was more important to her than them that she got the car back. Or maybe they were secretly hoping she wouldn't get it back at all and she'd have to rely on her mother for rides like she did when she was fifteen.

She headed downstairs to where her mom was fixing breakfast for Andrew and Kurt. Her father had slept on the pull-out couch in the den. It was the first time he'd stayed at the house since the separation. She stopped in the hallway and listened for a moment, wondering if they were talking about her. They weren't.

"How long is the flight to Sydney?" she heard Andrew ask.

"About seventeen hours," their father said. "Please don't talk with your mouth full."

"It's shorter to go *from* Sydney *to* San Diego because of the tailwind, isn't it?" Andrew asked.

"That's exactly right," their dad said proudly. As Candace lurked in the hallway listening, she couldn't help but feel a pang of sadness. She'd become used to his absence, and hearing him now felt like a reminder of when things were better. *What a strange way to end this*, she thought. *One last morning with everyone together before I never see these people again. Bizarre.*

Candace entered from the hallway.

"Hi, sweetie." Her mother smiled, trying to be pleasant. "Want me to make you some eggs?"

"I'll eat at school," she said, disgusted at her mother's attempt to pretend everything was fine and this was just another normal day. Candace glanced over at her father, who didn't look up at all. At least his awkward reaction was an honest one.

Her dad abruptly stood. "Hold up there, honey. I'll

drive you. It's on my way out of town anyway." Candace bit her lip, digesting the bad news. She'd figured this would be their plan. He was going to drive her to school to make sure she didn't bolt. *Pathetic*, she thought. *Do they really think I can't skip school? I've done it before.*

Both Candace and her father were silent on the drive. She'd figured the entire ride would be one long lecture about how irresponsible she was and how she made her mother worry and how she could've been killed. It wasn't.

"I want you to get your car back today" was all her father said. She'd figured that after the pizza outing, he and her mom would want to know more about where she'd been staying and who had possession of the car, but surprisingly, they hadn't asked.

"I'll have it back by lunch. Avery's taking me to pick it up from our friend's house," she lied. Her dad simply nodded.

She had no idea why he wasn't demanding answers to all the questions her parents had, but he wasn't. Had she disappointed him so much that he just didn't even bother? Maybe now that the secret was out about her being adopted, he didn't need to pretend to care anymore. Deep down, she hoped that wasn't it.

Part of her wanted to grab her father's hand and tell him she was sorry for running away, sorry that she'd been such a terrible daughter, sorry that she couldn't be the perfect child in the way Andrew was. But that apology was too difficult, and so Candace just sat quietly, letting the air from the vent blow against her face.

As Candace's father pulled up to the curb in front of her school, he sighed. Candace glanced over at the building and all the kids going in. In a weird way, she was going to miss it. She wouldn't miss Ian or that loudmouth Joey or any of the teachers who were always on her case about one thing or another. But she would miss checking in with Avery between classes and helping to decorate the lockers of freshman on the first day of school, and singing along with the other students at the pep rallies. She'd miss dressing up for homecoming and the excitement she felt when the last bell of the day would ring. Those things, at least, had been fun. Even so, school was part of her old life. She was looking forward to the new one—the one in which she woke up each morning in Toby's bed and spent her day doing anything she wanted.

"I know you don't want to go in there, but it's not going to be that bad," her father said. Candace realized she must've been frowning a little and he misread her thoughts.

"Actually, it is." She said it as if she were really considering going in.

"Who cares what anyone says? You're a smart, beautiful, strong young lady. In one year, you'll graduate, go to college, and you won't even remember half of these kids' names. Keep your eyes on the prize. Don't let anyone pull your attention away from that."

Candace looked over at her father and nodded. She felt guilty deceiving him, letting him believe she intended to go to classes. But then she thought of Toby, and the freedom she would have once she reunited with him.

She opened the door and got out. Candace walked toward the entrance but instead of going in, she ducked behind a column and waited for her father to cruise off down the street. As soon as he turned the corner, Candace came back out, jogged across the street, and began to walk in the opposite direction.

She was almost to the end of the block when she heard Avery yell, "Candace!" Candace didn't break stride as she turned to see her best friend hurrying toward her.

"I gotta go!" Candace yelled back. "I'll call you later!"

Thirty minutes later, Toby's truck pulled into the parking lot of the strip mall where Candace was sitting on the curb, playing a game on her phone. She heard him honk twice, and when she looked up, she could see him behind the wheel, a broad smile plastered across his square jaw. Jumping up, she ran over and stretched into his window to kiss him.

"Welcome back, beautiful," he said as she pulled away. "Get your cute little ass in the car where it belongs."

Candace lounged on the sofa in Toby's living room, flipping through a magazine. She was enjoying the lack of studying, school, or having to do anything of importance. She still felt a tinge of guilt for the ruse she'd pulled off earlier that morning. Her parents had no reason to trust her at all anymore, but they had. Her father had dropped her off at school believing that she would sit in class and listen and do all the things diligent students do. She didn't deserve to be trusted and she knew it. For that, she felt bad. But what could she do? There was no way she was going back to face all the questions and jokes about her being adopted. No way she'd risk being separated from Toby again.

Her parents simply didn't understand what it was like to be in high school. How kids, if they wanted to, had the power to make a person's life hell. Like poor Meghan Horan, the mousy little freshman made a target by her last name. Candace wasn't sure who started it but someone had come up with calling her Meghan Whore-On and whenever her named was written someplace, kids would write "her back" or "her knees" afterward. When the dean's list came out and the names were posted, Candace had seen that someone had written "the motel bed" after Meghan's name. Later that day, Candace heard someone sniffling in one of the bathroom stalls. When she peered underneath, she recognized Meghan's worn black wedge sandals. Candace had knocked and asked if everything was okay. When Meghan mumbled a half-hearted yes, Candace had decided not to press. She already knew why Meghan was upset and aside from encouraging her to legally change her name, there was nothing she could do to help her. The real world—the adult world—was bigger. If someone broke up with a boyfriend, no one had to know. The person could still go to work, go out and socialize, and it didn't follow them around. School was different. *Your boyfriend breaks up with you and you're forced to watch him kissing your replacement in the hallway six days later,* Candace lamented. *Everyone knows everything about everybody, and it feels like people are always looking for ways to bring each other down a notch.* Even though Candace wished she could ignore it all, the idea of being on the receiving end of that sort of meanness and gossip bothered her.

That was one of the things she liked about Toby. None of that petty high school stuff mattered to him. He had bigger things to worry about than who dumped who, how quickly they'd moved on, and whether or not someone was adopted. He had real worries—adult worries. He had his cousin to deal with, rent to pay, a business to run. He was above all the bullshit.

She looked over at Toby, who was counting cash out on the coffee table. He looked so serious. *Damn, he looks good when he's focused like that*, she thought. But he also looked a little menacing. She wondered what he'd be like if he ever got really angry. There was something in Toby that made her think he could be violent if someone set him off. She saw it in Keenan as well. Being

bounced around from place to place, beaten uncon-
scious by your stepfather . . . that had to have an effect.
It had to turn someone hard. And yet he had this amazing capacity to be gentle and sweet and even vulnerable
with her. That dichotomy made her feel closer to him.
It made her feel safe. She knew he'd never unleash on
her physically, but if someone ever hurt her, she was
sure he'd go after them.

"So what happens if people don't pay you back the
money they borrow?" she asked, curious.

He ignored her at first, trying to keep count. Then
he glanced sideways at her with a grin. "Why? You
thinkin' of stiffing me on the grand you owe?" He was
teasing.

"No," she said dramatically. "I was just wondering. I wanna understand what you do a little better."
This peer-to-peer lending stuff didn't make a whole
lot of sense to her. There had to be a reason why people would choose to borrow money from someone like
Toby instead of going to a bank or just getting a new
credit card like her mom did when the dishwasher
broke and she needed money for a new one.

Toby avoided eye contact with her and started to
count again. His silence bothered her.

"You don't break their legs or something, do you?" she said, making it seem like a joke even though the thought had crossed her mind.

"Have you ever broken your leg?" he asked flatly.

"No."

"It's not as big of a deal as you think."

Candace gasped. Toby smiled, liking her reaction.

"I'm kidding!" he said, giving her a little push. "Relax. Stop with the silly questions so I can count here."

Candace laughed, but deep down she felt like there was something Toby wasn't telling her. Whenever she asked him a serious question about what he did, or how he made money, he turned it into a joke. It worried her that he felt he couldn't be completely honest about that part of his life when he'd been so honest about the other parts. But she didn't want to make the mistake her mother made and nag and press and obsess over it. No. She knew how it felt to be on the other end of that. She would just be cool and in time, he'd trust her enough to let her in on all the details. Before she could say anything else, her cell phone rang. She looked at the display, instantly excited when she saw it was Mike Foster calling.

"It's that detective guy!" she said, and answered the phone.

"Well?" Toby asked as Candace hung up the phone. He knew it had to be good news because Candace could barely contain her excitement. "Did he find her?"

"He wouldn't say. He just says he has good news and he wants us to come to his office." Candace leaped off the sofa and threw her arms around Toby. "I can't believe this!"

Toby wanted to share in her enthusiasm but was skeptical. "Why couldn't he tell you on the phone? That's weird to me." The mere thought of this guy exploiting Candace's need to find her biological mother and screwing her over pissed him off.

"I don't know!" Candace said. From the look on her face, he could tell she was scrambling to come up with a reason. "Maybe she wants to meet me in person and it's going to be a surprise! He said it was good news! Oh my god," she said as she sat back down. "I can't believe this. Is this even real? Am I going to meet my real mom?"

Toby smiled, letting go of his suspicions. He was glad to see her so happy. "Well, let's head over to his office." In a frenzy, Candace grabbed her purse, threw on her hoodie, and was out the door.

Toby did the same. There was no way she was going without him.

Less than an hour later, Candace and Toby sat in Mike's office, waiting for the man who was about to deliver on the promise of finding her mother. She felt sick to her stomach, nervous and excited and worried all at once. *This is it*, she thought. *Today is the day I get to find out who I really am.*

She knew the information she was about to receive was going to change her life forever. Everything was going to be different from this point forward. She squeezed Toby's hand.

"You okay?" he whispered. She nodded, even though she felt far from okay.

Mike returned and dropped a file onto his desk as he sat down. "All right," he sighed. "First off, you had an *open* adoption."

"What does that mean?" Candace asked, thinking it sounded better than whatever the alternative was.

"Your natural mother had the option to contact you, but she apparently didn't. Her name is Callie Tressor."

"Callie Tressor," Candace repeated, as if she needed to say the name herself to make it real. *Callie Tressor.*

She repeated it again in her head as she looked over at Toby. A million questions were rushing into her brain. She had no idea where to start so she blurted out the first one she could actually get a grasp on.

"Does she live in LA?"

"I don't know. I couldn't find an address for her. She evidently got evicted from her apartment in Eagle Rock several months ago." Eagle Rock? That was part of Los Angeles. Only about twenty miles from where Candace had been living. Had she been so close for all these years?

"I don't get it," Toby said. "How is this good news? I mean, it's good to have a name and all that, but Candy wants to actually meet her."

Mike opened the folder and slid it to Candace. She looked down at a series of photos of an attractive guy with black hair and a gym body as he retrieved mail from a mailbox. They looked like creepy surveillance photos and clearly, Gym Guy had no idea they were being taken.

"Who's this?" she asked.

"Vance Tressor," Mike said. "Your brother. And I do have *his* home address."

The afternoon sun had just begun its descent when Candace pulled up in front of the address Mike Foster had given her. It was a small house, well kept, but old. An older-model sedan sat in the driveway. Candace remained in her car, trying to calm the butterflies in her stomach. Rubbing the palms of her hands together, she exhaled slowly. What if her mother screamed at her to leave? What if they pretended not to know who she was when she introduced herself? What if, by now, her mother was dead? She looked back down at the photos of Vance. He didn't look mean or anything, she concluded. He looked just like a normal guy getting his mail. Still, she had no idea how he'd react. Did he even know he had a sister? Would he want one?

Candace thought about a saying her father often repeated: *You can't put the meow back in the cat.* There are certain things that, once they're said or done, there's no taking them back. It applied here as well. *If I go up to that door and make my existence known, there's no going back.*

She thought about what she'd said to Toby after he asked if she wanted him to come along.

"I can wait in the car if you want," he'd offered. Candace was pleased he'd asked, but in her gut she knew this was something she had to do alone. Toby exuded toughness. She'd seen the way he'd eyed Mike Foster suspiciously when he told them he couldn't find her mother's address. Toby was just protective of her, she knew that, but she was afraid his attitude might put Vance off. Her brother might be more likely to talk to her if she went alone.

Reminding herself that she'd come too far to turn around now, she threw open her car door. With resolve, she marched up to the front door and rang the bell as the butterflies fluttered into her throat. After a few moments, the door opened and Vance stood before her. He was the guy in the photos and she knew the second she saw him that he was, indeed, her brother. She could just feel it. There was a connection. A tinge of excitement shot through her.

"Yes?" he asked politely, as if she were selling Girl Scout cookies or something. He obviously had no idea who she was.

"Hi," she said nervously. "My name is Candace and . . ." She couldn't get the rest to come out. *Dammit, I should've practiced this in the car*, she scolded herself as he stared at her, confused. "God, this is so much more awkward than I thought it would be," she muttered under her breath. "I'm Candace and . . . I'm pretty sure I'm your sister."

As soon as the words left her mouth, a look of surprise and recognition came over Vance.

"Wow," he said. "Uh, yeah. Uh, come on in." She could tell from his smile that he'd been waiting for this day to come. He opened the door wider, inviting her in. Candace followed her brother inside.

FOURTEEN
AN UNEXPECTED RECEPTION

Candace sat across from Vance on an old sofa that looked like it had worn out years ago. The room was clean but barely decorated; in addition to the sofa, there were two chairs that didn't match, a coffee table, a wide-screen TV mounted on the wall with a new Bose sound system, and a bookcase. Vance just stared at her with a smile on his face. It helped assuage the tension Candace was feeling.

"I wondered if you'd ever come looking," he finally said.

"I would've come sooner," Candace said, scratching

at the label on the bottle of soda Vance had given her. "But . . . no one told me. I didn't know I was adopted." Her voice oozed with resentment.

He just nodded. "Wow," he said. "This is surreal. I remember when you were born. I was there. At the hospital."

"You were?" she asked, surprised. *This is incredible*, she thought, feeling like she'd found a piece that finally fit into the crazy puzzle that was her life. For seventeen years, she'd assumed her mother and father were there for her birth. But they weren't. Vance was. Vance remembered the day she came into the world.

"I was five years old. Living with our grandmother at the time. Our mom's mom, not our dad's."

Our dad, he'd said. That must mean they shared the same father. "So are you and I full—?" she asked, hopeful.

He nodded. No way!

"How many others . . . ?" Candace asked, imagining that maybe she had some sisters, too. Would they look like her? Would they have her big brown eyes and long hair? She'd always wondered what it would be like to have a lot of sisters and brothers.

"Just the two of us," he responded. Then Vance

stood abruptly. "Hang on a sec," he said, and hurried out of the room. Candace sat there, looking around, feeling increasingly more comfortable by the moment. *I have a brother,* she thought. *A big brother. Not a half-, or a step-, or an adopted brother. A full brother, and he's excited to see me.*

Vance returned with a tattered photo album and a handful of loose pictures. He set the book down on the coffee table and handed her the photos. They depicted a man with dark hair like Vance's and dark eyes like hers. He had handsome features under his beard and he resembled Vance.

"That's our dad," Vance said, and pulled a photo from the stack of the man leaning against a motorcycle, holding a helmet under his arm. "This is the last photo taken of him before he died."

"He's dead?" she asked, her voice cracking. Candace felt a mix of emotion. She was looking into the face of a man she was too late to meet in person. *Someone should have told me sooner. Their lies cheated me out of the chance to see what he was really like.*

"When did he . . . ?" She turned one of the photos over. There was a name and a date scribbled on the back: *Marty, May 2000.*

"He, uh, he died in prison . . . of a heart attack. Before you were born," Vance said slowly, as if remembering that she had never heard any of these details before.

At least it was before I was born, she thought. Even if she hadn't been given up, she never would have known him anyway. "What was he in prison for?"

"Manslaughter. He got into a brawl in a bar and . . . a guy ended up dead. I don't know all the details."

Candace looked back down at the photo, taking in the news.

"He wasn't a bad guy," Vance assured her. "He just . . . He didn't always make good decisions. Especially when he drank. Mom said the guy he got into the fight with hit his head on the ground and . . . he never intended for him to get that hurt, I guess." Candace studied Vance as he continued to talk. As he went on, she realized there were a lot of gaps in his stories. Things he didn't know about their father either.

"But you remember him?" she asked.

He nodded. "A little bit. Like I remember *that* day." Vance pointed to the photo in her hand. "It was taken at a Memorial Day barbeque. The whole neighborhood was there and one of the people had a swimming pool in their backyard. Dad swam with me." It sounded odd to hear him refer to this man as "Dad." That word had only ever been used to refer to Kurt.

"Do you have any of our mom?"

Vance forced a smile and opened the scrapbook. He pointed to a photo of their mother, Callie. In the picture, she was holding a martini glass and smiling with her arm around another woman. Candace studied her slight, thin figure and long, light brown hair, trying to find a resemblance. There wasn't much of one, really, at least not in this picture.

"She was about twenty-five there. It would've been right before she got pregnant with you." Vance stood. "I may have some that are more recent that never got put into an album. Let me check."

As he walked down the hall, Candace sat back and looked around the room. She felt overwhelmed by it all. If she hadn't been adopted, this might've been her home too. She pictured herself sitting on the sofa doing homework and watching television with Vance. *Life would've been so different*, she thought. Better? Worse? She had no idea yet. She was still piecing it all together, forming new scenarios in her mind of what it would have been like. She was glad she felt so at ease with her older brother, but she was still concerned about her mother. Vance hadn't said much about her since she arrived.

"What's she like? Our mother?" Candace asked as Vance returned with a more recent picture of their mother.

Vance sighed. "I don't know what you're imagining, but she's not, you know, exactly what you might expect. She never finished high school. She moved around a lot, job to job."

Candace shook her head and studied the photo of her mother standing by a Harley Davidson chopper. *Now there's a connection*, Candace thought, tracing the motorcycle with her finger. She guessed maybe her mother liked bad boys too. "It doesn't matter. I don't care about that kind of stuff." Candace let go of the grandiose images she'd had of her natural mother's life. Callie Tressor wasn't some Beverly Hills celebrity or high-powered international CEO. Who cared? Callie Tressor was a regular person who'd had two children, gave one up for adoption, and had been married to a guy named Marty who died. Candace wasn't disappointed that her mother was who she was. In fact, being with a real person was preferable to all the appearances

Shannon was so determined to keep up. Especially after the divorce. Appearances, Candace had learned, was just another word for lies. Lies about how they were all fine and happy even when they weren't.

Candace wouldn't live like that. And now, standing in front of her biological brother, for the first time in her life, Candace felt rooted. She was no longer floating haplessly through a cloud of discontentment. She was anchored and strong and part of something bigger than herself.

"I was about to make dinner," Vance said. "Do you want to stay?"

"Depends on what you're having," Candace teased. Vance's smile showed that he liked her sense of humor.

"Steak and lobster. We eat it every night," he quipped back.

"Then, yeah. I'll take mine medium-rare."

Vance chuckled and handed her a package of pasta he had retrieved from the pantry. As Candace opened the package, she thought about how while the conversation was heavy, the mood definitely was not. They were honestly having fun. It felt, for Candace, like they'd grown up together as brother and sister. There was a comfortable familiarity that seemed to just exist without effort, like they'd been making dinner together their entire lives.

"So how long was she pregnant with me before he died?" Candace asked, wondering about their father.

Vance thought for a moment as he set up the cutting board and began to chop tomatoes. "Only a few months, I guess. Dad passed away in . . . I think it was November. . . ."

"So she was six months along." Candace did the math as she filled a pot to the brim with water and set it on the stove.

"What the hell is that?" Vance asked, chuckling.

"This is what we call *water*," she responded, feeling perfectly at ease being a smart-ass. "What does it look like?"

Vance grinned. "It's gonna boil over in half a second. Haven't you ever cooked before?"

The truth was, she hadn't. Her mom always did the cooking and all Candace had ever made using the stove were grilled cheese sandwiches and French toast. Smirking, she took the pot back to the sink and dumped some of the water out. "You're kind of a know-it-all . . ." she said under her breath, but loud enough for him to hear. He laughed.

"I've been cooking my entire life. I *should* know it all by now. I'm actually really good at it."

"Oh yeah?" she said, teasing. "Let me know when your episode of *Top Chef* airs."

"Ha-ha," he said. She giggled. He mimicked her laugh, making her laugh even harder. They stopped when they heard the front door open.

"That's Mom," he said softly. Candace's heart leaped up into her throat, and that familiar hot feeling surged through her stomach. She had no idea how her mother would react to seeing her standing in the kitchen, unannounced, making dinner with her newly found brother.

"Sure you want to do this?" he asked. "Back door is right over there."

Candace nodded, mute. This was her moment. No way was she giving it up.

A second passed before she stepped into the doorway. Candace gasped. She didn't expect her mother to look the way she did. Callie was incredibly thin, her pale skin stretched over her frame and peppered with bruises. Candace could barely pry her gaze from the dark circles under her mother's eyes. Were they from a lack of sleep or the remnants of yesterday's mascara?

Any vision she'd created of her mother being a regular person—maybe someone who worked at a bank or an insurance company—was gone. There was no way her mother wore the stained shirt with a ripped collar to any type of job.

She's a drug addict, Candace realized as Callie nervously began to twirl her greasy hair on a bony finger. That's when true disappointment sank in.

"Mom," Vance said carefully. "This is *Candace*."

Callie looked from Candace to Vance and back, giving nothing away. "How old are you?" she asked slowly.

"Seventeen," Candace said, and waited for a reaction. There wasn't one. Callie just stared at her with a blank look in her eyes before exhaling.

"I don't know any Candace," she muttered, and then shuffled past them down the hall. With tears welling in her eyes, Candace watched her disappear around the corner. That was it? That was all she had to say to the daughter that she gave away? Candace was sure Callie understood who she was from the way Vance had said Candace's name. To just pretend she didn't know Candace was gut-wrenching. If she'd said that she didn't want to see her, or that she was too surprised to know what to say, Candace would've understood. But to act as if she were just some random teenager who Vance met on the street and invited in for dinner was . . . cruel. Candace had prepared herself for a mother who would be surprised that she'd sought her out, but she couldn't have expected *this*. Seeing the pain on Candace's face, Vance quickly put a hand on her back reassuringly.

"She's wasted right now," he said. "Let's just give her a little time to sober up while we eat and then I'll go talk to her, okay?" Candace nodded but she couldn't fight the sobs that came from so deep inside her that they hurt. Covering her face with her hands, she began to cry. *It's my own fault*, she thought, *for believing that I could be happy and feel like I belong. I won't ever belong.* Callie's crushing dismissal left her feeling even more lost than before.

She felt Vance put his strong arms around her and hug her to his chest. His warmth felt good. "Hey . . ." he said in a soothing voice. "Don't let that hurt you. She's said some pretty awful stuff to me, too. And this is all going to be okay. There's just . . . a lot of things you don't understand." His words made her feel a little better. She needed to trust that things couldn't get worse. And they couldn't. Could they?

The mood was solemn for both Candace and Vance as they ate dinner.

"Does she ever talk about me?" Candace asked.

"No," he said softly, shaking his head. "But you have to understand how Mom is. She's her own worst enemy. And it's not just the pills and booze."

"What do you mean?" Candace asked, trying to ignore the hurt she was feeling after hearing her mom never mentioned her.

"She's so . . . I don't know. She'll never admit she made a mistake about anything. Even when it's obvious. Stubborn."

Candace looked past Vance toward the hallway. "Do you think she'll be that way with me?" she asked.

"She's that way with everyone. Even me. She needs rehab. She's needed it for years."

"You can't make her go?" Candace had never known anyone who needed rehab before, but it seemed pretty clear to her that their mother did.

"Uh, no. I could force her by turning her in to the cops . . . but she said she'd never speak to me again." Vance's words were laced with pain. Candace felt bad for him.

"You believe her?" she asked, finding it difficult

to wrap her head around the idea that a mother could disown her son for doing what was obviously best for her. "Would she really stop talking to you? After she's sober she'd probably see things differently." All Candace knew about addicts came from television shows, and the people on them rarely held a grudge once they were clean.

"It's why I haven't done it . . . yet," he said, looking down. There was a note of shame in his voice. "I've spent hours and hours researching and talking to people, but you know . . . it's just complicated." This was all so far from what Candace pictured. The moment Mike Foster told her she had a brother and showed her the photos of Vance, she had begun to create a fictional life for him, imagining what it had been like for him to be the one who hadn't been adopted away; who had the chance to build that mother-child bond; who had the *normal* life. She was beginning to see that Vance's life was far from normal. No, he'd never had to wonder who his real mother was or feel the betrayal Candace felt when she discovered she didn't belong in the family she'd always thought was hers, but he had his own collection of demons that he'd come to accept. Maybe life had been just as unfair to her brother as it had been to her. . . .

"Do you think she's going to come out and talk to me tonight?" she asked.

Vance exhaled slowly. "I think . . . you should give it some time. Let her have a few days to process it and decide what she wants to say."

Candace sank back, disappointed and angry. A few days? She'd had seventeen years to ponder what she'd say to the daughter she gave up.

"I don't think I can do that," Candace said. How could she possibly get in her car and leave without having a conversation with the woman who held so many of the answers to her questions? She needed to know who Callie was, what her father was like, why she was given up but Vance wasn't. She couldn't just walk out. It had taken a crap-ton of courage to just step up to Vance's door. She wasn't going to give up that easily.

"Let me go talk to her," he said, and stood.

Candace heard him knock on Callie's bedroom door. Then she heard it open and shut. She got up and slipped down the hall so she could eavesdrop. "You should talk to her, Mom," she heard Vance pleading.

"Nothin' to say." There was something else but Candace couldn't make it out.

"Really?" She heard Vance raise his voice. "You've

got nothing to say to the daughter you gave up? How about telling her about the birthday gifts you bought but never sent? Or the time—"

"It's none of your business! Stay out of it!" Callie responded, irate. Candace closed her eyes, trying to stave off the sting she felt about hurtful remarks she was overhearing through the flimsy wooden door.

"That's your answer for everything. It's not my business. Except it is! *You're* my business! Your life has been one regret after another covered up with booze and pills and whatever else you can find so you don't have to feel bad. This is your chance to change all that. Right now. For once, do something that's hard to do. Not for her, but for yourself!"

Candace bit her lip. There was a long pause. Vance's words hung in the air like a dense fog. She hoped the silence meant Callie was reconsidering.

"I got nothin' to say." Callie's words rang with a resigned finality. Tears brimmed in Candace's eyes.

"You're unbelievable," she heard her brother say before opening the door. Startled to see Candace standing there, he let his shoulders drop.

"I'm sorry," Vance apologized. "She needs time."

Candace was livid. "I don't understand why she

can't just talk to me! I'm not asking for anything. Just to see what she's like!" Being stubborn was one thing; being unreasonable was something entirely different!

Vance put up a hand, trying to calm her. "It's not about that. She just pushes aside things that are difficult."

"Well, I'm not gonna be pushed aside!" Candace declared, and muscled past her brother and banged on the door with her fist. "I borrowed a thousand dollars to find you! That's how bad I wanted to know who you are! And I'm not leaving here until you talk to me!"

The words came out like a rush of white water. Candace poured out her fear, anxiety, and desire for acceptance. She didn't expect Callie to respond to her any differently than she'd responded to Vance, but she couldn't leave without trying. And it was important for her mother to know the lengths she'd gone to just so she could see her face-to-face. She half expected Callie to tell her to go screw herself. Just like Toby said might happen. If she kicked her out of the house, Candace knew her only choice would be to leave. She couldn't risk her mother calling the cops on her and being hauled back home again.

She's never going to talk to me if I yell at her through a door, Callie surmised. *What am I doing? I should've just given her time like Vance said. I've probably screwed everything up, just like I do everything else.* But as Candace beat herself up over her decisions, she was shocked to see the doorknob begin to turn.

Candace stepped back, speechless, as Callie opened the door. Staring into her mother's face, she could see years of misery in the woman's cold, pained eyes.

"Fine," Callie said. "Let's talk."

Toby, still dripping wet from his shower, adjusted the towel around his waist as he hurried to the bed and snatched up his ringing cell phone. Hoping it was Candace telling him how the initial meeting with her brother had turned out, he was surprised to see a number he didn't recognize. *Maybe her phone died and she's calling from his phone*, he thought.

"Hello?" he answered.

"I'm calling for Tobias. Did I get the right number?" The woman's voice on the other end was tired but hopeful.

"Who's this?" he asked. No one called him Tobias. There was a pause. Then . . .

"My name is Shannon," the woman said. "I'm

Candace's mother. Please don't hang up. I know she's with you."

Toby's jaw tightened. "She doesn't want to talk to you. Just leave her alone."

"I'm not going to *leave her alone*," Shannon spit back. "I'm her *mother*! And if you think—"

Toby hung up on her. Assuming she would call right back, he quickly blocked her number from his phone. *This woman never freaking gives up*, he thought as he pulled a clean shirt from his dresser and slipped it over his head. No wonder she drove Candace crazy. Running away twice should've been enough of a clue that Candace wanted to be left alone, but Shannon couldn't seem to respect that. It was apparent that if he and Candace ever wanted to live in peace, he was going to have to find a place far away from Shannon.

Toby dropped his towel and slid on a pair of boxers before falling back onto his bed. He wondered how things were going with Candace and her brother. He hoped this guy wasn't a prick to her. And if he was, he hoped Candace wouldn't tell him or he'd feel compelled to drive straight over to the guy's house and kick his ass.

Toby wondered if he'd made a mistake by

encouraging Candace to find her biological mother. It was what she wanted, so he wanted to give that to her, but he hadn't spent much time thinking it through on his own. The best thing for both of them would be to move far away and start a new life someplace else. Candace could be rid of Shannon's control and he would be able to escape his past. He hoped this brother and mother—if she were alive—wouldn't end up encouraging Candace to stay in LA.

San Francisco sounds cool, he thought. *But it's just as expensive as LA.* Maybe someplace in Oregon or Arizona. He knew a guy who'd moved to Phoenix. *Maybe we can shack up with him for a little while. Or maybe Vegas. Vegas would be a blast.* All these thoughts of moving away with Candace made Toby smile. He'd been longing for a new beginning for quite some time. It had come in the form of Candace. *I'm not going to let anyone keep us apart*, he promised himself. *Not Keenan, not Candace's newly discovered brother, and definitely not Shannon.*

Candace sat across from Callie, who fidgeted nervously as she spoke. "You have your father's eyes," Callie said, studying her hard. To Candace, who blinked back a tear, it seemed like more of an observation than a compliment. She felt Vance's comforting hand on her shoulder.

"What do you want to know?" Callie asked awkwardly.

"Everything!" Candace blurted out, as if it were the most obvious answer in the world. "Starting with why you gave me up."

Callie took a moment and it seemed like she was putting some real thought into her words. "Your father was sentenced on a Friday. The following Monday, I found out I was pregnant with you. I already had a four-year-old son I didn't know how I was going to take care of. I knew you'd have a better life with someone else." Her voice was flat and devoid of emotion, and that's what made it even more difficult for Candace to hear.

"Why didn't you ever try to find me?" she asked as a tear broke loose and ran down her cheek. "Didn't you even care how I was doing?"

"I knew where you were," Callie responded. "I saw you a few times. I went to your ballet recital . . . sat in the park when you had your sixth birthday party there."

"You did?" Candace was surprised. "My adoptive mother said she didn't know where you were."

"She didn't," Callie assured her. "She had no idea I

was there." There was a bit of relief in finding out that her mom hadn't lied about that, at least. She truly didn't know Callie. But why would this woman give her up and then secretly come to important events? It made no sense.

"But I saw how happy you were, kissing and hugging your mother. I saw how she and your dad went to all that work to plan games and decorate, and get you a cake and presents . . . I saw how much they loved you and how happy it made them to give you that party, and I knew I wouldn't have done it." Callie shrugged, reinforcing her apathy.

Candace didn't want to believe that. Every parent wants to see their child happy. She was sure Callie would have done the same. Maybe not to the extent that her parents did, because she didn't have the money, but she would have done something to mark the occasion. "Know what?" Candace asked, clasping her hands together. "I don't think that's true. I think you would've given me the same things they did—"

"No. I wouldn't," Callie interjected quickly. "Ask Vance. Think he ever got a birthday party? One. And that's because his aunt Kendra threw it for him when he was seven. I showed up late." Callie looked at Vance, who glanced away. "Every time I saw you happy," Callie continued, "it made me feel worse. Not because I *couldn't* give you that, but because I knew I *wouldn't*."

They all sat in silence, unsure where to go with the conversation. It dawned on Candace that between her and Vance, maybe she was actually the lucky one. Yes, he'd grown up knowing who his real mother was, but a childhood with Callie didn't seem anything to envy. It wasn't just that Callie couldn't afford all the things many parents can. It was that she simply didn't care to put in any effort. The notion that people could have children and then not want to create all the fun memories that they could with them was beyond Candace's comprehension. She had so many great memories of her childhood: the pizza outings, the family vacations, waking up Christmas morning to find Santa eating the cookies she and Andrew had left for him.

For the first time, Candace realized that those things took effort on her mom and dad's part. Like how her mother had hired someone to dress up like Santa and surprise them. For months, Andrew had bragged about how he'd caught him in the act.

She thought about all the money her parents spent on new school clothes each autumn, and annual trips to

Disneyland to celebrate the end of summer. Vance never got anything even close. *Maybe*, Candace thought, *I was actually lucky that Callie didn't raise me. That she made the decision to give me to someone else.*

Finally, Callie spoke. "I know you want me to say that giving you up was the hardest thing I ever did, but it wasn't. It was easy. I knew you'd have a better upbringing, and my life would be easier if I wasn't always disappointing you."

Tears began to stream down Candace's face. She wiped them away with her sleeve. She felt herself getting angry. That telling feeling that always came right before she lost control and said whatever she could come up with to hurt the other person.

"You could have at least contacted me," she said, her voice getting louder.

"Why?" Callie asked, still calm.

"So I'd know who my *real mother was*!" *What is wrong with this woman? Is she insane? Doesn't any of this make sense to her?*

"You have a real mother!" Callie blurted back, showing emotion for the first time. "One who loves you very much and did a wonderful job raising you! I saw it with my own eyes! At that party, with that little boy in one arm, cutting cake with the other . . . giving out little bags of candy to all the kids, putting bandages on scraped knees . . . I saw a woman who loved being a mother, who loved her kids. And inserting myself into that didn't make sense. When I saw how much your parents loved you, I knew I did the right thing, and doing anything to complicate that would've been . . . wrong."

Callie reached her pale hands under the coffee table and pulled out a little gray box. She opened and removed a yellowing, weathered invitation. Handmade, it had *You're Invited to Candy's 6th Birthday Party* written on the front, and round plastic beads, made to look like pieces of candy, decorated the sides. Every detail had been added with care. Callie held it out to Candace; she took it.

"I found it in the trash after everyone left," Callie muttered softly. Candace stared at the eleven-year-old invitation in her hand, lovingly made by her mom. A river of confusion, pain, and guilt swirled inside her. Inside the invitation, along with the date, place, and time, her mother had written *Our darling baby girl is growing up!* Candace choked back a sob.

FIFTEEN
A PERFECT PLAN

"I need your answer, man." Keenan leaned against the kitchen wall, waiting for Toby to answer. "You in or out?" Toby knew the time had come for him to make a decision about whether he was going to take part in the plan Pedro had put together. Twenty-four hours ago, he might have declined, but the call from Candace's mother had been weighing on him the past few hours.

There were too many things here in LA that threatened to rip him and Candace apart, including the less-than-legal lifestyle he'd been sharing with Keenan, and Shannon's attempts to bring her daughter home. She had his cell number. She'd probably searched

Candace's phone records to get it. And if she'd done that, she'd probably also talked to the private detective they'd hired. Or maybe she'd gotten hold of the police report that jackass cop filled out when he arrested him. Toby wasn't sure but regardless, it was only a matter of time before Candace's parents showed up at his door with the cops claiming he was harboring a runaway. To truly have a life with her and be the guy she deserved, he was convinced they'd have to move away and they'd have to do it soon.

The only way out was to do this deal. Yes, it was risky, but the money he'd make would be the start they needed. And that's why Toby decided that this would be the *last* job he'd ever pull. After this, he'd go completely straight. He'd head up north, get a job in construction, work his way up to foreman, save enough for a little house, and give Candace the life she deserved.

"All I have to do is *drive*, right?" Toby asked, still trying to mitigate the risk in his mind.

"That's what I said," Keenan responded, hopeful that his cousin was coming around. Toby waited a few seconds to respond. He was waiting for one last warning from his gut, but it never came. He had to conclude that this was the best course of action.

"Yeah, I'll do it," Toby said with conviction. Despite

the inherent risk, committing actually made him feel relieved. He now had a plan and he could move forward with it.

A broad smile came over Keenan's features. "Smart choice, bro. This is easy-ass money." Toby knew that was a lie. There was nothing easy about robbing a drug dealer, but the money part was true. "You didn't say nothing to your little *chica*, did you?" There was concern in Keenan's voice.

"Of course not. She doesn't know anything about this and I don't want her to."

Keenan nodded, pleased. "I'll let Pedro know you're on board and we're good to go."

"When are we doing this?"

"Gotta talk to Pedro, but he was thinking tomorrow."

Toby nodded. Tomorrow. Good. He wanted more than anything to get this done with so he could focus on more important things, like leaving all of his and Candace's LA problems behind.

As Keenan ducked out of the kitchen, presumably to call Pedro and tell him the good news, Toby glanced out the window and suddenly stopped. Stretched across the very bottom corner of the frame on the other side of the screen was a thick, densely spun sheet web. Propping his elbows on the counter, Toby leaned down and saw a black widow spider nestled behind the chaotic mass of silky strands. Huddled in the cool darkness, she would have been hard to see if it weren't for the tungsten light of the kitchen reflecting off the bloodred mark on her glossy black abdomen.

This is an omen, Toby thought as a sense of dread settled over him. A night breeze slipped in, causing the web to vibrate. The spider remained dead still, silently waiting for the next unsuspecting insect to blunder into her trap. Had he made a mistake in telling Keenan he'd be a part of their plan? Were they as naive as the fly that couldn't see the deadly black widow lurking behind the mesh of gossamer threads?

Toby stood up straight, pushing the poisonous thoughts from his mind. If he let those ideas seep deeper into his brain, they could sabotage the entire job. He had to remain confident that the three of them could pull this off, that Dawson would never know who to blame, and that no one would get hurt or busted. He had to visualize himself behind the wheel, shoving the SUV into drive and peeling away with Pedro and Keenan inside, the case of cash in their grips. With explicit detail, he imagined Pedro dividing up the cash and handing each person their share. He could almost smell the scent of crisp bills, the sound they made as he thumbed through the packs.

Sitting down at the table, Toby pressed his fingertips into the scarred wooden top as he let his mind carry the thoughts even further. He pictured himself surprising Candace with a diamond ring in a small velvet-lined box. He'd keep the ring box hidden in his pocket as they stood at the base of picturesque Multnomah Falls just outside of Portland.

"Where are we going?" she'd ask, and flash him her perfect smile.

"You'll see," he'd say as he parked the truck, took her hand, and began to lead her through the mass of orange and red autumn foliage toward the hidden waterfall. As they got closer, they'd be able to hear the crash of the icy water as it cascaded down the rocks. He'd take her out onto the bridge where they could feel the chilly mist against their faces. Once they were there, he'd get down on one knee and pull the box from his pocket. Her gloved hands would fly to her mouth and he'd see that look of surprise and happiness that danced in her eyes.

Then he'd ask her to spend the rest of her life with him.

Toby savored the fantasy for a moment, holding on to an image that had never crossed his mind before. Marrying Candace. He had no idea how he could be having these thoughts, but he was. He felt like he'd known her for a lifetime.

He pulled his cell from his pocket and searched for images of Multnomah Falls. He had been there once as a child, when his grandmother had loaded him into the car and drove up to Oregon for a funeral. He couldn't remember who had died but he thought it was one of her friends. They were only there for two days, but before they made the fifteen-hour drive back to Los Angeles in her old Buick, she'd stopped at a McDonald's, bought them each a kids' meal, and drove them to the waterfall. It was the first and only time Toby had ever seen one and he was mesmerized by the sheer magnitude of it.

As he scrolled through the photos, he decided that it was most definitely a place he wanted to take Candace. And with that thought firmly implanted, the sense of foreboding that had come with the discovery of the spider passed. Any doubt that clouded his mind was gone and he was sure he'd made the right decision. This would be his last crime, and then he'd embark on his brand-new life with her. *I can do this*, he told himself. *I'll do this for Candace*.

SIXTEEN
A DIFFERENT APPROACH

Under a full moon, Vance and Candace walked down the cracked driveway to her parked car. As he opened the door for her, an autumn breeze picked up and Candace could feel a chill. She got in and rolled down her window. Vance leaned in, resting his head on his forearms. She could tell he was concerned for her.

"So, you okay? I know that's probably not what you wanted to hear."

"I don't know what I was expecting, to be honest," Candace said. "I just feel . . . sort of lost right now."

It was an understatement. Three days ago, she

thought she was a normal teenager living with her natural parents and annoying little brother. Two days ago, she didn't know who her parents were, only that the people she believed in and trusted since she was a baby had deceived her. Today, she discovered that she had a brother, her natural father had died in prison, and her mother was an addict who didn't regret giving her up. On top of all of that, the conversation with Callie only made her feel guilty about how she'd been treating her mother, not just in the past few days but for months.

She wasn't sure why her mom was so hard to get along with, or how the ultra-contentious dynamic between them took hold, but it did. Despite her epiphany that perhaps her mom loved her more than she'd realized, she knew that going back home would just lead to more tension and fights like it always had. The irony is that Candace knew she was more like Shannon than she was Callie. At least she hoped so. Even though her mother had a temper and could be bossy and overbearing, it was better than the apathy she saw in Callie. She couldn't imagine how Vance had dealt with it all these years.

"I'd probably feel a little lost, too," Vance said, and smiled. "I would like to spend more time with my little sister, though. Maybe meet this boyfriend of yours." It was exactly what Candace needed to hear. Vance welcomed her into his world and wanted to be a part of hers.

"Meet my boyfriend? You sound like a protective older brother," she teased.

"Maybe I am," he said, and grinned.

"I'd like to meet Monica, too." Monica was Vance's girlfriend of almost three years. Over dinner, he'd shown Candace a picture of her.

"Cool. When are you gonna come back and see Mom?" he asked.

Candace exhaled, "Think she even wants me to come back?"

Vance nodded. "I do," he said. "Baby steps."

"Then maybe you could invite me over for dinner on Sunday night." Candace smiled broadly.

"You're invited," he said. Her connection to Vance was undeniable. He seemed like he could end up being a lifelong friend.

Ready to go back to Toby's and process all that had happened, she turned the key in the ignition. Instead of starting up, she heard a loud and unfortunately familiar whining noise. Candace threw her head back in frustration.

"Ugh. Not again."

"Sounds like your starter's going out," Vance said, and motioned her to turn the key again. She did and the engine started right up. "Why don't you bring it into the shop tomorrow and I'll look at it?"

"Shop?" Vance had mentioned earlier that he was a mechanic, but he hadn't told her exactly where he worked.

"Sorry, guess that's an important piece of information. Corbin Automotive and Body over on 43rd. About a mile east of here." He pointed behind him giving her a vague sense of how to get there. Finding the place wasn't the problem though.

"Will you take an IOU?" she asked, knowing she couldn't afford to pay him to fix the starter. At least not at the moment, but she'd add it to the grand she already owed Toby and pay them both back later.

Vance grinned. "I'm not gonna charge you, silly. Family discount." She exhaled, relieved and touched. "Drive safe, kiddo."

"Thanks. See ya tomorrow," she said, and shifted into drive. As Candace drove away, she snuck a glance at Vance, who stood in the weedy yard, watching her. *That's my big brother*, she thought happily. Somehow that thought led her to thinking about Andrew and how worried he probably was. During her short stint at home, she'd promised that they'd have a heart-to-heart, but they never did. She didn't even finish playing pool with him at the pizzeria. *I suck. I need to be better to him. I need to play some of his silly games and not get so mad at his pranks and actually talk when he wants to talk.* Then it dawned on her that if she stayed with Toby, any chance of proving to Andrew that she could be a better sister than she had been, was gone. And that, too, added to her feeling of being lost.

Images of the party Callie had brought up popped into her mind. It was especially hot that year and her parents had spent hours before the party filling up water balloons in the kitchen sink for a water balloon fight. She'd had so much fun. She remembered hitting her father square in the chest with a water balloon that soaked his entire shirt.

Maybe that's why Candace felt so betrayed when she found out she was adopted. Maybe Candace wasn't angry that they had lied as much as she was angry that she wasn't really theirs. She wasn't one hundred per-cent sure why she felt so much resentment toward her mom in particular. Her mother loved her. The effort she had put into that birthday party was undeniable. Her life with them before the family broke up, before she'd found out she wasn't theirs, had been pretty great. Certainly better than Vance's life was with Callie, and even better than a lot of her friends'. She'd thought Callie would be her salvation. Now, everything was opposite.

Once again she wasn't sure where she belonged. If she stayed with Toby, she'd never have the chance to do any of the things she should've done differently when it came to her mom, dad, and Andrew. But if she went back to them, her parents would discourage her from seeing Toby. *Is this what being an adult is like? Finding myself in situations where I'm screwed no matter what choice I make? The allure of being a grown-up is kind of deceptive*, Candace thought as she merged onto the freeway. She'd waited so long to be able to have control over her own life and now she wasn't sure which doors to open and which ones to shut.

"How'd it go?" Toby asked eagerly as soon as he saw Candace walk in the door. The television was on but he hadn't been paying attention to it. His thoughts had been on Candace, the robbery that was going down tomorrow, and a better future in Oregon. Candace kicked off her shoes and plopped down next to him.

"I need a beer," she said.

He handed her his. It was still cold. "That bad?" he asked, and shut off the TV, giving her his undivided attention. Whatever had happened, she wasn't nearly as much of a mess as she was the first night they met, so he figured it couldn't be that bad.

"I have a brother who's really cool, but the rest . . . I don't know how I feel about anything right now." *What does that mean?* Toby wondered. It was obvious that she didn't want to go into detail even though he would've listened to whatever she had to say. He hated being pressed when he didn't feel like talking about something, so he didn't want to put the same pressure on her.

"That's okay. You don't have to," he said as he noticed the little invitation in her hand. "What's that thing?"

She held it up and looked at it, some of the aging glitter falling into her lap. "An invitation to my sixth birthday party. My mom made it."

Confused, Toby said, "I thought she gave you up when you were just a baby. . . ."

"Yeah, she did. I meant my adoptive mom. Shannon," Candace clarified, and took another sip of beer. Toby deflated a little. That was the first time he'd heard her refer to anything Shannon had done without a note of contempt. He hoped things weren't so crappy with her biological family that she was considering heading back to Shannon's house. The very thought of it made him uneasy.

"She, uh, called my cell, by the way. Looking for you. I hung up on her," he said. He was hoping Candace would say *Good! Maybe that'll teach her never to call here again!*, but she didn't. Candace didn't say anything, just looked at him with a conflicted expression. "You're okay with that, right?" he asked, suddenly unsure.

"I don't know. I feel like I've been kinda hard on her," Candace said, staring at the invite. Toby could feel panic rising in him.

"No you haven't," he quickly chimed in, taking her hand. "Look, if you talk to her, she's just gonna try to convince you to go home. She'll make it impossible for us to see each other. That's not what you want, is it?"

Even as he said the words, Toby knew that he was being selfish. But no. He wanted Candace to stay with him, to run off with him and start a new life, and he absolutely refused to entertain the idea that maybe being home with her mother was actually the best thing for her. Every objection Shannon could come up with—that Candace needed to graduate high school, that she needed to be in a safe environment, that she needed to be taken care of—he would make sure those things happened. The more he'd thought about it, the more he was convinced that he could give Candace everything she needed to be happy.

He could only imagine the fit Shannon would pitch if she knew Candace was dating a guy who was twenty-three.

This sucks, Toby thought. He didn't want to give her up. He was falling in love with her and the life they'd shared for the last few days: falling asleep in each other's arms, sleeping late, making breakfast, hanging out during the day, partying at night. His entire future somehow hinged on Candace now. He absolutely could not handle it if she moved back to her house in the suburbs.

When Candace just looked down at the invitation again, he could tell she was missing her mom. "I know I tease you a lot and stuff," he said with sincerity. "But I like having you here. I don't want you to go." Those were tough words for him to say. He took such pains to keep his feelings private. He felt more at ease when she smiled at him. God, how he loved that sparkle in her eye.

"The way I feel about you, I haven't felt that way in a long time. Maybe not ever," he said, unable to look at her as the words spilled out. It was like a window to his heart had opened just a crack and he could finally articulate what he'd been feeling.

She put her beer down, reached over, and laced her fingers in his. "I'm not going to leave you," she said. "No matter what."

"Would it freak you out if I said that I think I might be falling in love with you?" he asked, feeling like that twelve-year-old boy once again, the one who was head over heels for Cara. When she didn't immediately answer, he flicked his gaze up to look into her eyes.

"No," Candace said gently. "That wouldn't freak me out at all. I'm falling in love with you, too."

As soon as she said it, Toby felt a wave of peace wash over him and the anxiety he'd been feeling was almost completely gone. He leaned in and kissed her full, round lips, letting his tongue dip into her mouth. His heart swelled in his chest, and as he tangled his fingers in her long hair, tilting her head back so he could kiss her more deeply, he wanted nothing more than to do this for the rest of his life.

"Come on," Toby said, and stood up. "Let's go to bed." As Candace let him pull her by the hand off the sofa, she felt as if she were going to burst with joy. Toby had just told her he was falling for her and now that they'd put their feelings out into the open, she no longer had to wonder what was going through his mind. Never in a million years had she expected to fall in love with a gorgeous bad boy like Toby. And even more surprising, she'd never expected someone like him to fall for her. But there was a connection there, a real connection that she'd never experienced before, and she knew she'd never be able to let it go.

When they entered his room, he peeled off his shirt and let it drop to the floor. Then he slipped hers off as well, kissing her again as they fell onto his mattress.

"You're beautiful," he whispered. Candace was so caught up in the moment that all she wanted to do was please him. Lightly kissing his strong chest, she worked her way up to his neck which still bore the faint scent of his cologne. She could feel his hands sliding up her back where he unhooked her bra. Once again his hands were threaded through her hair and he pulled her close, their chests pressed against each other as they kissed. *I love this guy so much.* The emotion of meeting Vance and Callie pushed far out of her mind. It would all be there for her to worry about tomorrow.

Tonight is all about me and Toby, she thought. *There is no one else in the world.*

SEVENTEEN
LIES AND CONSEQUENCES

Toby was careful not to wake Candace when he got up, and pulled on a shirt and jeans. Even as he stared down at Candace sleeping peacefully on his pillow, enjoying the way the light played across her hair, he couldn't shake the nervousness he felt about the robbery he and his cousin were about to pull off. It was nothing new. Toby always felt anxious before pulling any sort of job—even the small ones—and he knew that a shot of whiskey was what he needed to calm his nerves.

Tucking his T-shirt into the waist of his jeans, he went out into the kitchen to finalize the details with

Keenan. His cousin was already seated at the table, looking over a map and eating cereal out of a plastic bowl. As Toby grabbed a bottle of whiskey from the cupboard and poured a shot into a coffee cup, Keenan began to enthusiastically explain what would happen.

"So," Keenan said. "Pedro's boy found out that everything is going to be at the warehouse for one day only."

"Everything?" Toby asked, pouring coffee grounds into the coffeemaker.

"Cash and drugs. The warehouse is right here." Keenan pointed it out to Toby on the map. "Near Cudahy."

"There's gonna be guys guarding that shit," Toby said. In Toby's opinion, this was the biggest problem. It wasn't breaking into a warehouse or getting out of there and back onto the freeway quickly, it was the surprise that lingered behind the heavy metal door. No drug dealer leaves that much cash and money unattended, so he knew there had to be guys—armed guys—there guarding it.

"Only one," Keenan said, raising his index finger for emphasis. "That's the beauty of it. Pedro and I walk in there with our nines pointed in this guy's face and walk out with all of it."

As Toby stood over the map, listening to Keenan explain the best getaway route, his mind drifted to thoughts of what Candace would say if she knew what he was about to do. Would she call it quits on him? Could she ever understand that he was doing this for her? He wasn't sure, but in a matter of hours, it wouldn't matter anyway. The deed would be done and he'd be packing up the truck to head north.

"Are you listening to me?" Keenan asked, annoyed. "This is important."

"Yeah, yeah, I hear you," Toby said, and poured coffee into his cup, letting it mix with the booze. "We get on the 710 at Firestone and go north. But stay off Atlantic. It's too obvious."

As Keenan traced the route with his finger, giving Toby side street options, the two men looked up and saw a sleepy, wild-haired Candace standing in the doorway. She was wearing one of Toby's T-shirts that hung way too big on her tiny frame. Their conversation instantly ceased, which Toby was sure looked awkward and suspicious.

"Am I interrupting something?" she asked.

"No," Toby said, trying to sound normal as Keenan rolled up the map and walked out. "I was just gonna make some breakfast. Want some?" He couldn't help but feel guilty hiding what he was doing from Candace. Still, for her safety, it was better she didn't know.

"Sure," Candace said, and walked over to the cupboard where Toby kept the cereal.

Wanting to prevent any further conversation about what he and his cousin were doing, he asked, "So, what're your plans today? Gonna go see your bio mom again?"

"No. My brother, though. He said I could bring the car in and he'd fix the starter." Toby nodded, too preoccupied to really listen. "I was thinking maybe I should call my mom—my other mom, Shannon—just to let her know I'm okay."

That got Toby's attention. He was sure opening communication with Shannon would lead to convincing Candace to go back home. "Do you think we could talk about that before you do it?"

"Aren't we?" she asked. "Right now?"

"I can't," Toby said, conflicted. "I have to leave. Keenan and I are . . . gonna go help out a friend." He knew it sounded like a lie but he wanted to keep it as vague as possible.

"Oh, all right," she said. She seemed put off by the ambiguity.

"We'll talk this afternoon, okay?" he assured her, trying to assuage his own nervousness and guilt. She nodded and he kissed her forehead. Keenan poked his head in and motioned for Toby to hurry up.

"We gotta go, cuz," Keenan said.

Toby turned back to Candace and kissed her again, more passionately. "Everything's going to be just fine." Even though he was saying it to her, he was really saying it aloud for himself.

He saw the confused look Candace gave him, but ignored it. Instead, he downed his coffee, picked up his wallet and keys, and walked out in silence with Keenan.

As Candace finished her cereal alone in the kitchen, heavy thoughts weighed on her. There was something decidedly different about how Toby was acting this morning and she was sure it had to do with Keenan. Keenan was trouble, and she hated the idea of that spilling out onto Toby. She thought about calling his cell phone and telling him that whatever he was doing, he should just turn around and come home. *I can't tell him what to do*, she admonished herself. *He's an adult. He has to make his own decisions.* Still, she didn't like being lied to and she had a strong suspicion that Toby wasn't telling her the truth about helping a friend. At the very least, when he returned later, she planned on having a frank discussion with him about honesty. Their relationship was less than a week old but if they were going to be together, they had to promise to tell each other everything.

It would be fine. Besides, she had more immediate concerns. Candace headed back to Toby's room, yanked a pair of jeans from her bag, and slipped them on. Then she pulled on a plain gray T-shirt, twisted her long hair up into a messy bun, and went out to start her car. Hopefully Vance would be able to fix the problem without too much trouble. She couldn't believe he was willing to do it for free. There had to be something she could do for him to return the favor.

Candace twisted the latch on the glove compartment and foraged through the pile of paperwork and junk inside. Sure that there was a list of what the mechanic had fixed previously when her mom had taken the car in, she was determined to find it. It could be helpful to Vance. As she scooped out old assignments and manuals and hair ties, she came across a little box of matches. The name of the restaurant, Vittadini's, was embossed in gold.

They hadn't been to Vittadini's in a long time. She

must've had the box in her room or purse and grabbed it up at one point and left it in her car. Candace remembered the last time they were there and she'd picked up the matches on her way out. It was for her mother's birthday three years ago. It was just her, her mother, and Andrew. Her father had missed it.

Candace pulled a fragile matchstick from the box and scraped it along the striking side, watching as the tiny phosphorus head burst into flame. She thought back to that night, remembering that she and Andrew had gone shopping together and bought their mom a bottle of perfume for a gift.

"Thank you." Her mother had smiled as she opened the bottle and sniffed the fragrance. "I absolutely love this. You couldn't have picked out a better gift."

"What did Dad get you?" Andrew had asked as he dug into his caprese salad. Their father was away on a long flight to Guam and couldn't attend Shannon's birthday dinner.

"Your father doesn't need to get me anything. I'm just glad the two of you are here with me to celebrate." Her mother's answer had satisfied Andrew, who turned his attention back to stabbing the tomato on his plate, but Candace had seen the sadness in her mother's eyes.

Her mom never once missed her dad's birthday, she thought. Her father always took his own birthday off to go fishing with his brothers and he'd always come home to a homemade German chocolate cake waiting for him. It was his favorite, and her mother would always get up early that morning to bake it.

Candace blew out the match and stared at the last wisp of smoke as it drifted into nothingness. She'd always blamed her mother for driving her father away, but perhaps the divorce wasn't entirely Shannon's fault. Maybe her father wasn't the best husband and maybe her mom got sick of it. *There are two sides to every story*, Candace thought. She'd been so resentful toward her mom that she'd never taken the time to think about it from her perspective.

Candace tucked the mess of papers and junk back into her glove box. She left the little matchbox on the console. As Candace turned the key, the starter made that familiar grinding noise like it wanted to start but couldn't quite make it happen.

"Come on," she pleaded with it. "I'm taking you to get fixed right now. Just work one more time. Pleeeeeeease." No dice. The car absolutely, positively wouldn't start. Frustrated, she plucked her cell phone from the console, looked up the name of the garage, and dialed the number.

Two rings and a cheery voice answered, "Garage. This is Monica."

"Monica!" Candace was happy to hear her brother's girlfriend on the other end of the line. Perhaps he'd already mentioned the situation to her. "This is Candace, Vance's newly discovered sister. . . ." She heard Monica's lighthearted laugh on the other end.

"Oh, hey! Vance said you were going to bring your car in today. I'm looking forward to meeting you." It was exactly what Candace needed to hear. It made her feel just a tiny bit better.

"Thanks. I was going to do it right now but it's refusing to start again so . . . I guess I need to have it towed." Candace felt a little embarrassed that she couldn't even manage to get the car to the shop.

"That's no problem," Monica assured her. "We have a tow company we work with a lot. I'll send a truck out right away."

"*That* would be awesome," Candace said before giving Monica the address to Toby's house. With that, she hurried back inside to take a quick shower before the tow truck driver arrived.

Warm, soapy water swirled around Candace's feet and into the drain. Much of the anger Candace had been harboring felt as if it were washing away too. *Things just aren't so black-and-white*, she thought. *People aren't perfect. They have flaws and make mistakes and they can't always predict the outcomes of their actions.*

"It's just not how life is," she found herself stating. Candace had always held everyone to such a high standard, assumed that everything everyone did was thought out and preplanned. She'd been looking at it wrong. And she'd been living with so much resentment. Her brother had it figured out. Even though his father died in prison, his mother was a drug addict, and his sister was given up for adoption, he didn't seem angry.

And yet here I am, Candace thought. *Pissed off at everything.* What did she really have to be so angry about? Yes, she was adopted, but the reason she never suspected it was because her mother and father loved her as much as they loved Andrew. Sure, her parents were divorced, but what if that was actually for the best? She'd always blamed her mother for not getting to spend time with her dad. But when Candace really thought about it, her father wasn't around that much before the divorce, either. Maybe it was her mother who had put in the effort all those years and when she couldn't do it anymore, Kurt decided to leave.

How weird that it took finding her biological mother to realize she hadn't been very fair to her adoptive one.

Candace turned off the water and stepped out. Wrapping a towel around herself, another thought struck her. Even if she could mend the relationship with Shannon, there was no way Shannon was going to let her stay with Toby. Candace knew her mom was worried about her, but if she told her where she was, the cops would come to take her home.

An email would be best. That way, she could say the things she needed to say, but her mother couldn't demand to know where she was and who she was with.

Toby sat behind the wheel of Keenan's SUV while Keenan leaned over in the passenger seat, double-checking the clip of his semiautomatic handgun *again*. Toby had watched him do it at least three times since they got into the car, and he could tell his cousin was nervous. Why wouldn't he be? What they were about to do could get them all killed. If Toby could have turned to Keenan and told him that he'd changed his mind and wanted out, he would have. But it was too late to do that now. He'd made a promise and he wasn't going to pussy out. He just hoped that Pedro hadn't miscalculated—that all this was going to be as easy as Keenan believed.

They pulled up in front of Pedro's house and stopped. Pedro lived in a sketchy neighborhood just east of downtown Los Angeles where the windows on the houses were barred and the structures looked as beat-down as their inhabitants. Toby was surprised to see Pedro's three-year-old daughter playing in the front yard with a puppy. Pedro's wife, Maria, a beautiful Latina, looked on as she chatted on her cell phone.

When she saw the SUV, Maria smiled and waved enthusiastically. *She has no clue what we're doing today. Pedro kept it from Maria just like I kept it from Candace.* Keenan waved back politely and hopped out. Toby watched as Keenan approached Maria, gave her a kiss on the cheek, and then picked up Pedro's daughter and tossed her playfully into the air. The puppy bounced around at his feet.

Toby felt sick. He kept picturing that black widow in his house and he knew deep down, the moment he saw Maria and the little girl, that something was about to go terribly wrong today. *This is the last time*

I'm ever going to see them. The thought was so present, he couldn't shake it. He wasn't sure if he was just trying to find ways to try to talk himself out of it. He couldn't do that. He'd already committed and the plan was in motion. There was no backing out now. He decided to turn in the other direction and focus on a teenager and his father who were bent down under the hood of a muscle car parked in their driveway.

A few seconds later, Pedro exited the house with a backpack slung casually over his shoulder. He kissed Maria and his daughter, and then followed Keenan back to the vehicle. As soon as they had pulled the doors shut, Toby could see the faux happiness fall from their faces, replaced by serious concentration.

"All right," Pedro said. "Let's go do this."

Candace sat on the sofa with Toby's laptop perched on her knees as she waited for the tow truck. She sipped coffee as she struggled to compose an email to Shannon. *Dear Mom*, she wrote. *I'm sorry I ran away.* As soon as she typed the words, she decided to delete them. It wasn't how she wanted to start. There was a lot to say, a lot of apologies to be made, a lot of emotions to synthesize into words. On one hand, she was still hurt that her mother hadn't told her the truth, but more than that, the fact that her mother had put up with so much from her when she didn't have to struck a painful chord in Candace. Here was a woman who kept trying even though Candace showed little effort in return. That suddenly meant something, and it wasn't anything Candace had considered until she spoke to Callie.

The doorbell rang. Thankful for the interruption, Candace got up and opened it, revealing a uniformed tow truck driver with a clipboard. "Candace White?" he asked.

"Yes. You're here for my car," she said pleasantly. "Let me just get my keys." When she returned, she handed the man her keychain with the little silver shamrock on it and watched briefly from the door as he backed his truck up to her car and hitched it. She shut the door and went back to the couch to continue working on the most difficult email she'd ever tried to write.

Keenan's SUV pulled up in front of an abandoned warehouse in Cudahy. The windows were, for the most part, boarded up, and those that weren't had deep cracks that splintered their frosted glass. There wasn't a soul anywhere in sight.

"In an' out. Ten minutes and we'll all be a lot richer," Pedro uttered as he pulled a balaclava from his backpack and put it on. Keenan did the same. Both men checked their weapons as Toby glanced around, praying no unexpected visitors would pass by. Their identities hidden under nefarious-looking masks, Pedro and Keenan exited the SUV and walked cautiously to the warehouse's side door. Toby watched nervously as Pedro kicked the door open with his boot, destroying the flimsy lock.

As Keenan and Pedro disappeared into the warehouse, Toby craned his neck to see if anyone was coming from the other side of the parking lot. There wasn't. He glanced over at the dark blue sedan parked by the entrance. It was the only car in the lot. Toby hoped that meant that Pedro's contact was right—there was only one guy inside guarding the money and drugs.

Hurry up, Toby silently pleaded, wishing Pedro and Keenan would come running out the door so he could take off and be done with the whole thing. The longer he sat there, the more his nerves got to him. He drummed his fingers on the steering wheel, ready to shove the transmission into drive and peel away. *What's taking so long? C'mon, man . . . hurry the hell up. . . .*

Through one of the broken windows, Toby could see some movement inside. Toby leaned forward to see, but all he could make out was a person moving slowly. It didn't look like Keenan or Pedro, though. *Oh my god*, he thought. *That's got to be Dawson, or one of his guys. . . .*

Toby shifted in his seat, worried. What should he do? Should he go in? Warn them somehow? Honk the horn? But what if he was wrong? What if it was really Keenan and Pedro who had managed to get the drop on Dawson and they were stuffing the drugs and money into their bags at that very moment? He could screw the whole thing up by deviating from the plan. Toby's hand moved to the door handle as he contemplated getting out of the car and rushing inside. *No*, he thought. *Don't be impulsive. Stick to what Keenan said. Just be ready to drive when they come bailing out that door. Any second now—*

Pop! Pop! Pop! Three gunshots. Toby froze, horrified. *What the hell just happened in there?*

Toby's foot hovered over the gas pedal, ready to go. He looked to the door. Nothing. No Keenan, no Pedro. Dammit! Where were they? Had they been shot?

A moment later, the door flew open and Keenan came running toward the SUV. His left sleeve was soaked; blood running down his hand and onto the bag he held in a white-knuckled grip. Toby, with adrenaline coursing through his veins, slammed the SUV into drive as Keenan jumped into the passenger seat.

"Go! Go! Go!" Keenan yelled.

"Where's Pedro?!" Toby shouted, not sure what to do.

"He's dead! Just go!"

Toby smashed his foot down on the gas and the SUV squealed off around the building, kicking up gravel in its wake.

Pedro clutched his chest and felt the sticky wetness of his own blood. He could barely move, not because of the pain but because he couldn't feel anything below his chest. Breathing heavily, he saw Dawson's hulking figure lean over him and found himself staring straight into Dawson's cold, hard eyes.

"Pedro," Dawson hissed. "Where'd he go with our money?"

Pedro, unwilling to rat out his friend, just looked past Dawson at the dusty rafters on the ceiling, imagining ways that this could still end with him alive. Dawson pressed the gun harder into Pedro's cheek.

"I don't know," Pedro gasped, his breathing labored.

"Pedro," Dawson said, his voice low and steady. "You're about to die. Now you can tell me where your friend went and die knowing that your wife and daughter are safe . . . or you can refuse to tell me and die knowing you're the reason Maria and your little *mija* left this world in a horribly painful way. And I can assure you . . . I'll let them know you chose that for them."

Pedro's gazed moved to the window. He knew the SUV was long gone. Toby and Keenan weren't coming back for him. *This is the end*, he thought as they drifted in and out of focus, and then he imagined his daughter and her puppy playing in the yard. He knew Dawson meant what he said. There was nothing else he could do to save his own life, but maybe he could give his wife and daughter one last gift that they'd never know he gave them. And so . . . he whispered Toby's address.

Dawson, satisfied, straddled Pedro, pointed his gun in the dying man's face, and pulled the trigger.

Candace finished her email to her mother and sat back, rereading it. She'd ended it with *I love you and I'm sorry*. It was a long email, rambling in some places, and she'd told her mom things she knew she needed to say: her feelings about the divorce, that she'd met a great guy and what he meant to her, and how she'd found Callie and Vance. She even told her about how Callie gave her the invitation to her sixth birthday party. She signed the email *Candy* and then hit send. There was nothing she could do to change it now. The email was in her mother's inbox, waiting to be opened.

Candace sat back and thought about Avery. Candy had been kind of a bitch to her, putting her in the middle with all of this runaway stuff. Since she was on a roll with her apologies, she figured maybe Avery deserved one too. Candace dialed her friend's number, but when Avery's voice mail came on, Candace looked at the time. *That's right. We'd be in World Affairs right now. . . . What a boring class.* She pictured Avery taking copious notes as their teacher droned on about current events and geopolitics and a bunch of other crap that Candace couldn't care less about. Avery could be nerdy at times, but the image of her looking from the teacher to her notebook to the board and back, intently focused on ensuring she copied down every detail, made Candace smile. She loved that little nerd. She hoped their friendship wasn't over.

Candace ended the call and sighed. *Maybe I should write her an email. Or buy her something. What do I buy the best friend that I've been a shit to? I know!* Candace had an epiphany. On their last shopping trip Avery had found a pair of earrings she really liked from a boutique store on Melrose. They had sparkly blue stones and—

Suddenly, the front door flew open and Toby pulled Keenan inside.

"What the . . . ?!" Candace jumped up, reacting to the blood-soaked hoodie and Keenan's disturbingly pale complexion. Keenan, now shivering, dropped the backpack on the floor. Toby locked the door and helped his cousin to the sofa.

"Oh my god! What the hell happened?" she screamed to Toby as he ran into the kitchen.

Candace just stood there, staring at the blood that was pooling on the carpet under Keenan's arm. She couldn't take her eyes off it.

"Candy!" Toby bolted from the kitchen with a towel in his hand. "Put pressure on that!" he bellowed as he wrapped the towel around the gaping hole Candace just noticed in Keenan's arm. Candace heard him but she was having trouble comprehending. All she could see was blood. *Holy shit! There's so much blood!*

"Candy! Did you hear me?" Toby yelled. Candace managed to nod. *What was going on? Where had they been? Was that a bullet hole?* A million questions flashed through Candace's mind and she couldn't ask any of them. Everything was happening so fast.

Seconds after she placed her hand on Keenan's wound, the towel was already soaked crimson. When she pulled her hand away from the towel and looked at the sticky, thick blood that covered her palm, Toby grabbed her wrist and placed her hand down hard on his cousin's arm once again. Keenan winced in pain.

"Like this," Toby said with authority, and pulled out his cell phone.

"Call Cheryl," Keenan groaned. "She can sew it up."

Cheryl? Who's Cheryl? What the fuck is happening?

"You need a surgeon, not a nursing student!" Toby countered. "We gotta get you to a hospital, man."

"Did he get shot?" Candace finally asked, her voice shaking.

"No way," Keenan breathed, ignoring her question. "I told you no hospital."

"If we don't do somethin', you're gonna bleed out!" Toby yelled back at him. She watched as Toby hesitated, unsure what to do.

Candace looked back down at Keenan's arm and the blood that was oozing up through her fingers. She felt sick and scared at the same time.

"Toby," she uttered. "I think we need more towels." She wasn't sure what had gone down, but if there was one thing she knew for a fact, the blood-soaked towel that was on Keenan's arm now wasn't enough. The initial shock was over and the limited amount she'd learned during her health class's first aid unit was coming back. If someone is bleeding badly, put pressure on the wound and elevate it above the heart.

"Holy hell, it hurts," Keenan grunted as Candace gently lifted his arm over his head and onto the cushion. As Toby rushed down the hall to the bathroom for more towels, Candace turned her attention to Keenan's pained expression. She didn't know what to say.

"Call Cheryl," Keenan ordered her as he pulled his cell phone from his hoodie with his good hand. "Her number's in there."

Candace took his phone but she was shaking so badly, it was hard to scroll through the numbers.

"She's smart. She'll be able to fix this," Keenan explained in a voice low enough that Toby couldn't hear. Candace managed to scroll through the names on

Keenan's phone until she reached the Cs and saw there were two Cheryls.

"There's two. Which one—" Candace gasped and stopped midsentence when she looked up to see Dawson's huge six-foot-four-inch frame standing only a few feet away at the end of the hallway. She had no idea who he was or where he came from, but he was pointing a gun straight at her.

Keenan turned to see what had frightened her so badly. He immediately jumped to his feet in an attempt to get away but Dawson fired, hitting Keenan in the neck. Candace screamed in horror as Keenan slumped back against the wall, dead before he touched the ground. Just like that. Keenan was gone.

Frozen, she looked back at Dawson, who leveled the gun at her.

"Holy shit, holy shit," she uttered.

Candace didn't even know she was speaking until she heard her own voice. "Please, no, no, no," she begged. Candace raised her bloody hands trying to shield herself from the bullet she was sure was about to barrel into her. Her eyes flooded with tears and Dawson's image turned fuzzy.

Then something unexpected happened. Dawson

suddenly pitched forward. He dropped his gun as Toby blitzed him from behind. The two men fell to the floor, fighting for control of the gun. Candace had no idea what to do. She needed to help Toby somehow; she needed to stop this man who had just murdered Keenan. She spun around looking for something to hit him with but there was nothing.

"What the hell's going on?" Candace was shocked to hear Vance's voice on the other side of the front door.

"Candace!?" Her mother's voice! Her mother—not Callie, but Shannon—was with him! Thank god! She desperately needed their help but had no idea how to get to them. As she raced to the window to signal she was inside, she heard the gun go off. It was deafening. Candace threw her arms over her head and cowered behind the chair. As Vance and her mom continued to bang with their fists on the door outside, it dawned on Candace that she didn't know yet who'd been shot.

Oh god, please don't let it be Toby. Please don't let it be him. . . .

From her position on the floor, Candace could see the hulking monster that had broken into their house stand up. She gasped and threw her hand over her mouth.

No, no, no . . . he shot Toby. . . .

She watched as he looked at the door. She could tell he was considering blasting through it, shooting anyone who stood in his way.

Please, no . . . please don't hurt them.

The killer turned and ran down the hall from the direction he came. She could hear the heavy pounding of his feet against the old, creaky floorboards until they suddenly disappeared altogether.

"Candace!" she heard her brother call once more, before a loud bang sent the front door flying open. Vance had kicked it in. Her mother and brother halted abruptly, shocked to see Keenan dead on the floor and Toby, barely breathing, lying a few feet away.

Candace jumped to her feet and ran to Toby, who was gripping his chest. Blood was soaking his shirt. Candace made eye contact with Vance and her mother before falling to Toby's side.

"Oh god! Toby!" she screamed, and pulled his head onto her lap.

Vance lunged past them and ran toward the back of the house to make sure the intruder was gone. Her mother pulled out her phone and quickly dialed.

"Mom!" Candace gasped, relieved her mother was

there. She had no idea how she'd connected with Vance but it didn't matter. There were two people there who could take control of the situation. Candace, overwhelmed with emotion, couldn't think clearly.

"Help him, Mom," she pleaded. "Don't let him die."

"I'm calling an ambulance," her mother assured Toby. "Just hold on."

Candace gazed into Toby's eyes. She could see the fear and pain.

"Don't worry," she said, trying to calm him. "The ambulance will be here soon. We're going to get you to the hospital."

As her mother talked to the 911 dispatcher, Candace looked up to see Vance come into the room from the hallway. He walked over to Keenan and put his fingers on his neck to check for a pulse. Candace observed the defeated look on her brother's face when he couldn't find one.

As Candace glanced back down at Toby, she could see the blood was coming quickly, squeezing out of his chest with every labored breath, and he was on the verge of losing consciousness. She caressed his cheek, trying to comfort him, until she saw the blood begin to spray from his mouth in a light mist with every pained exhalation.

"Ambulance is on the way, buddy. Stay here. Keep lookin' at me," Vance implored, trying to get Toby to focus on him instead of the pain. Tears poured down Candace's cheeks.

Toby's eyes rolled back; his brain losing oxygen from loss of blood. Candace saw it and it sent another rush of panic through her.

"No, no, no!" she sobbed. Her mom put her arm around her as she finished answering the questions the 911 operator asked.

Candace noticed Toby's hands begin to shake and she grabbed one, squeezing as hard as she could. She could tell he wanted to say something to her but couldn't get the words out. As she looked into his eyes, she saw his gaze turn upward and his hand slipped from the wound on his chest. Candace let out a primal wail as Toby's body relaxed for the last time. He went limp in her arms.

Candace choked back her sobs. She felt her mother's hands gently pull her away from Toby. Candace gripped his jacket, unwilling to let go.

"Candy," her mom said. "Sweetie . . ."

Consumed with grief, Candace let Toby's hand slip from her fingers and she fell into her mother's embrace, barely able to breathe.

"It can't end like this, Mom!" she cried. "I love him! I love him! He can't die!"

Burying her face against her mother's shirt, Candace wept uncontrollably until the paramedics arrived and announced both Toby and Keenan dead at the scene.

EIGHTEEN
PICKING UP THE PIECES

"Candy?" The door to Candace's room opened abruptly without a knock. Candace rolled over and saw her mother standing in the doorway, her features tense. Candace rubbed her eyes and tried to push the nightmare of Toby's death from her brain. Every time she slept, for the past eleven nights, she'd been taken back to that horrible moment when Toby exhaled his last breath. The therapist her parents had found for her told her that those dreams would eventually go away, but they hadn't yet.

"What?" Candace sat up, knowing from the tone

of her mom's voice that she had something important to tell her.

"The detective just called. She said they've made an arrest and they want you to come down to the station to identify him." Candace's heart leaped into her throat and she thought for a moment she might throw up. Part of her was elated that they'd actually caught the guy who murdered Keenan and Toby, but the other part of her dreaded seeing his hulking, ugly face ever again. Every time she pictured him, it was the moment he'd pointed the gun right at her. He'd had a vacant look in his eyes, almost nonhuman. Candace never wanted to see that look again.

"I really don't want to do this," Candace said, even as she stood up and began to pull on a pair of shorts. "I mean, I know I have to, but . . . I just . . . I just want to get it over with."

Her mother nodded, understanding. "If it helps put him away for life, we need to do it."

"I know," Candace said, feeling more confident about it as she twisted her long hair up into a messy bun. "Did she say how they found him?"

"They actually caught him three days ago trying to cross into Mexico with a fake ID. I guess it took a few days to transport him back up here."

She could just picture that creep nonchalantly sliding his fake passport to the customs official, a smug grin on his unshaven face. She wished she could've seen how his expression changed when the official came back and slapped cuffs on him. That asshole must have been so surprised. Even better was the image in her mind of the killer sitting in a sheriff's bus, shackled at the ankles and wrists as he was driven through the harsh desert back to LA.

As Candace turned her attention back to getting dressed, she could see her mother studying her face, worried about her. "Mom. I'm okay. Really," Candace assured her as she slipped on a pair of flip-flops. "This is what I've been asking the universe to give me ever since it happened. Let's go."

At the police station, Candace and Shannon were met by Detective Lorraine Peters who, despite her small stature, led them down the corridor with an air of authority.

"So this is a typical lineup just like you've probably seen on TV a million times," the detective said, the badge on her hip pocket catching the light each time she turned and glanced back at them. "Five guys who all look kind of similar and you tell me the number of the one that did it. We'll all be behind one-way glass, so he won't be able to see us."

"Okay," Candace said, and followed Peters into a small dark room. The five men were already lined up, single file, waiting. Candace recognized the shooter immediately. He'd cut his hair differently but that was all. He had that same vacant look as he held the number 2 in front of his stomach and seemed to be gazing up at something past them. "Number two," she said with certainty.

"How sure are you?" the detective asked, and scribbled something down on a slip of paper.

"One hundred percent. That's the guy."

Peters smiled and handed her the slip to sign. The whole thing took less than a minute.

"That's all we needed," Peters replied with another smile. "This'll all be handed over to the DA now, so don't be surprised if someone from his office calls you."

"Do you think it'll be hard to get a conviction?" Candace's mom asked.

"Good lord, no," Peters retorted. "We have so much on this guy . . . and don't forget, it's not just two murders, it's three. We matched the bullets from all three victims to the same gun Dawson had hidden in his trunk when he tried to cross over. With your eyewitness account and all the physical evidence, he's going away for a long time."

"Thank you, Detective," Candace's mother said, relieved.

"Yeah," Candace added with sincerity. "Thank you."

As Candace and her mother sat at a window table of a coffee shop near the police station, Candace finally asked her mother the question that had come and gone in her mind for the last week and a half. She'd been so preoccupied with everything, including helping Toby's aunt Patricia plan a funeral for both Toby and Keenan, she hadn't thought to ask it. "Mom? When I was staying with Toby, how did you find me?"

Her mother exhaled and set her cup down on the wooden table. "Well . . . the first night, Andrew and I called around to all your friends and we drove around the neighborhoods looking for you . . . then, after you were picked up by the police and ran off the second time, I got Toby's old address from the police report. I went there, but Toby's ex-girlfriend—at least I think that's what she was—wasn't much help."

Candace looked down, feeling guilty as she listened to the effort her mother went through. "Then Andrew had the idea of printing off all the numbers you called from your cell phone, since our plans are all connected, and we started calling them. That led me to the private investigator."

"You talked to him?"

"I went to see him, actually," her mother said, sipping her latte. "He didn't want to give me any information but after I threatened to turn him in to the police for aiding a runaway, he changed his mind and gave me Vance's address. Callie didn't know where you were, but she figured Vance would, and so I went to talk to him at the garage and he said he'd just sent the tow truck over to get your car, so that was where we figured we'd find you."

Candace gazed at her mother, duly impressed and touched. "Wow. That was a lot of work."

Her mother thought about the comment for a moment, then gave her a warm look. "It's what mothers do for their kids. Someday, when you have your own children, you'll understand."

"I hope my kid's not a pain in the ass like I am," Candace said, grinning, trying to make her mom smile.

"Karma," her mother said, returning the grin and raising an eyebrow. "Maybe you should rethink having kids after all. . . ."

"You're probably right." Candace laughed. It was the first time since she'd lost Toby. "But then the question becomes what did you do as a teenager to deserve a kid like me? Come on, 'fess up. Your karma's not so great, either."

Her mom giggled and then turned serious once again. "Really, though. You're both good kids. I'm pretty lucky as a mom." As soon as she heard those words, Candace felt a wall between them crumble. She'd never connected to her mother in this way before. As she looked around the coffee shop at all the people lost in their laptops and books and cell phones, she no longer felt like the outcast—the adopted kid who didn't know where she belonged. She belonged here. Her family was hers and they weren't perfect, but whose is? And maybe she wasn't as difficult to love as she'd believed.

NINETEEN
A WORLD WITHOUT

"We need more balloons," Andrew said as he carefully tied a bouquet of shimmery green mylars to the back of a lawn chair. It was Candace's eighteenth birthday and four months to the day that Toby passed away.

"I think that's enough, don't you?" Candace asked, and gave her little brother a smile.

"Balloons are going to make this party," Andrew announced.

"Huh? I don't even understand what that means," she quipped as he disappeared through the patio door. Candace sat back and looked at the festive decorations set up around the backyard. There was a banner that read *Happy Birthday, Candace* and several tables with green tablecloths and little vases of white flowers.

Although Candace was happy to be celebrating her birthday with the people she loved, there was one very important person missing. She wished Toby could be with her right now, helping her mother set out the bowls of chips and side dishes, helping her father with the barbeque. She pictured him standing over the coals, laughing and talking to Vance as they cooked up the hot dogs and burgers. The time she'd had with Toby had been so short that she'd already cycled through the memories of things they'd done together a million times. To keep him alive, she had to picture him in situations he'd never take part in and with people he'd never had a chance to meet.

Candace looked over at Andrew, who was coming out the patio door with more balloons. Where did he get them all? He was followed by her mom, who brought out a beautiful white sheet cake iced with buttercream frosting and adorned with green and yellow flowers. As her mother set the cake down on the table, Candace walked over to check it out.

"That's gorgeous, Mom," she said, wrapping her

arm around her mother. In fancy script lettering *Happy 18th Birthday, Candy* was written across the top. Candace stuck her finger into the icing near the bottom and licked it off.

"Really, Candy?" her mom said, joking.

"Hey. It's my day, I can do anything I want," Candace joked back. When she saw her mother raise an eyebrow she decided to qualify it. "Within reason, of course."

"Happy birthday, honey!" They turned to see Kurt step out with a wrapped box.

"Dad!" Candace said as she gave him a hug. "I thought you had to work."

"I told them there was no possible way I could miss my daughter's special day, so they canceled the flight," her father said with a grin.

"Did they really?" Andrew asked, intrigued.

"No, sweetie," her mom said. "Don't you know your father's sense of humor by now?"

Andrew smacked his hand against his forehead, causing Kurt to laugh.

"Seriously, though, Dad, I'm glad you made it. It's a nice surprise." Candace was happy that her father had joined them for her birthday party. He hadn't done that since he moved out. She knew her parents would never get back together, but maybe they'd put some of their differences behind them the way they did when they joined forces to try to find her. Although Candace still felt bad for putting them through all that, maybe this could be the silver lining. They could move forward, at least a little.

Andrew took the gift from their father and shook it. "What do you think is in here?" he asked Candace with a gleam in his eye.

"Whatever it is, I hope you didn't just break it," she teased, taking the box away from him.

"I didn't," he assured her.

"You already know what Dad got me, don't you?" As soon as she said it, Andrew covered his mouth and laughed conspiratorially. "Maybe I'll have to pin you down and tickle the crap out of you until you tell me. . . ."

Andrew made a cross with his fingers, holding it up to her as if shielding himself from a vampire. "Stay back!" he yelled, and ran back into the house.

"He takes after you," their father said jokingly to Shannon as he grabbed the apron from the picnic table and slipped it over his head, ready to start up the grill.

Candace laughed as her mother grinned and shook her head. For a few joyful moments, Candace was in the present, her mind far away from the loss of Toby.

As her parents went back inside to get more food, Candace received a text from Avery: *Sorry I'm late. On my way now!* it read. Candace smiled.

Get your ass over here now! Candace typed back, and followed it with a winky emoticon.

She laughed when she got Avery's response: *Take it easy, birthday bitch.*

"Let's get this party started!" She turned to see Vance come out through the patio door holding hands with Monica. Her other hand loosely held a pink gift bag with a white bow that matched her white spaghetti-strap dress.

"Vance! Monica!" Candace first hugged Vance and then threw her arms around Monica's tanned shoulders. "I'm so glad you're here!"

"Happy birthday!" Monica said, and lifted up the gift bag. "Where should I put this?"

"I'll take it," Andrew announced as he snatched it from her hand. He hurried over to the gift table and set it down with the others that he'd already painstakingly arranged.

It felt surreal to see Vance and Monica at her parents' house. As her mom came out and offered everyone something to drink, Candace quietly observed their interactions. Since Toby's death, everything had felt so thin and hollow. Even though the police had caught and arrested Dawson, Candace couldn't manage to feel enthusiastic about anything. She'd returned to school, sleepwalked through her classes, and felt pretty much empty most of the time. Today was the first day she actually felt happy. Happy that her new brother and his girlfriend were forming connections with her mom, dad, and Andrew. This strange family of hers was coming together. They were all getting to know each other and she was at the center of it.

"There's a surprise coming," Vance whispered into Candace's ear with a grin. She gave him a perplexed look until she saw Callie step through the door. She was wearing a new blouse and matching skirt, her hair was clean and pinned up, and she balanced a dinner plate with a homemade, albeit a bit uneven, chocolate cake. Candace gasped, shocked to see her there.

As Callie looked around uncomfortably, Candace's mother greeted her warmly and led her over to the table where the green-and-white cake already sat. Shannon inched it over to make room for the small, homemade cake Callie had brought.

"I should've guessed you'd already have a cake," Callie said, regretful. "And look how beautiful it is, too." Callie's cake was far from the spectacular bakery cake Shannon had ordered. Candace presumed Callie's came from a box you buy at the grocery store, but she was still elated to have it there.

"I'm glad you brought chocolate," Shannon reassured her. "This one's vanilla, so now everyone has a choice." Candace smiled, appreciative that her mother was going to the effort to help Callie feel at ease. She'd been so welcoming of Vance and Callie into their lives. It meant a lot to Candace. Since the day Toby died and Candace moved back home, things had been different between them. Instead of seeing all the things in her mother that she also hated in herself, she saw a completely different person. Her mom had gone through hell to find her. *What determination that took*, Candace thought. *How much do you have to care for someone in order to do that?*

Candace had thought that maybe her mom would try to dissuade her from hanging out with Vance and Callie but she hadn't at all. She'd invited them over for dinner a few times, even though Callie never accepted. Vance, on the other hand, happily showed up each time with a bottle of wine and ate seconds of her mom's cooking, sometimes thirds. Andrew was always impressed with how much Vance could eat.

Candace was shocked that Callie actually showed up. When she'd invited them, Callie had originally told her that she wouldn't be there. Candace wasn't sure why she'd changed her mind. It didn't matter. Candace gave Callie a warm hug.

"I'm so happy you decided to come," she said. Callie smiled shyly.

"Me too" was all Callie said as she went to twirl a lock of hair, but realizing it was all up in a pin, she quickly wrung her hands.

"I have something to show you," Vance whispered to Candace. She noticed that Andrew had pulled Monica over to the very back of the yard near the fence and was pointing out something that probably wasn't very interesting in the grass.

"I know what it is," Candace said, excited, and motioned for her brother to follow her inside.

In the kitchen, Vance pulled a tiny box from his pocket and opened it. Inside was a beautiful solitaire engagement ring. Candace clapped softly, trying to contain her giddiness.

"When are you going to do it?" she asked.

"I don't know," he said nervously. "I haven't decided yet."

"I'm telling you! The top of the Ferris wheel at the Santa Monica pier. It'll be awesome. Oh wait! No! You should win her a stuffed animal or something and then have it in the bear's mouth or something."

"What if I don't win anything, though?" Vance said with a chuckle. "I can't stand there all night trying to knock down cups and stuff."

Candace laughed. "Do you suck that bad?"

"Nerves," he explained.

"Okay, okay," Candace said. "The Ferris wheel is your best bet." Candace turned in time to see Andrew and Monica walking toward them. "Hide it! She's coming in!"

Vance quickly tucked the ring box back into his pocket before Monica could catch a glimpse of it.

"Your mom said she needs you to bring napkins out," Monica said sweetly.

"Got 'em," Candace replied. She grabbed the napkins and headed back out to the party with Monica and her two brothers.

Looking at the cakes side by side, Candace felt complete for the first time in a long time. She had two mothers, two brothers, two families, and eighteen years after her birth, they had finally come together. Most people see their eighteenth birthday as a celebration of their arrival into adulthood, Candace thought as she gazed over at Callie helping her mother with the iced tea, Vance tossing a miniature football to Andrew, and her dad chatting with Monica behind the smoke of the grill. The end of being a child, and the start of an adult life with freedom, new opportunities, and responsibility. Weird how everything changes so fast. In the last year as a "kid," she'd lost herself, found love, lost someone she loved, gained a new family, and finally found herself all over again.

As difficult as it was to remember how it felt to lie in Toby's arms, their time together, though short, would always be with her. In the days after his murder, she'd driven several times to his quiet house and just sat in her car, staring at the crime tape that stretched across the door. She'd closed her eyes and imagined it the way it had been a week before when it was full of people, full of life. Part of her found it hard to accept that she could never open that front door and see Toby sitting on the sofa, playing poker with his cousin and drinking a beer.

None of them, herself included, would ever set foot in that house again. Those memories had become woven into her, stamped on her soul like a tattoo.

Toby's life may be over. But mine is just beginning. If there was one thing she'd learned, it was that life is fragile. She vowed to make every day count and treat the people she loved with care because they could be gone in the blink of an eye or the sound of a gunshot. Her quest to find Callie had started with the need to find herself. *But I already know who I am*, Candace realized. *I'm the person I choose to be.* The past didn't matter. What mattered was how she was going to take what she learned and move forward. Candace wasn't sure what the future held, but she no longer felt lost. She no longer felt like a child. She felt like a woman. And whatever the future brought, she was ready.